# THE BEGIN...

Connie & Isaac

Book 3 in
The Blue Butterfly Series

D H Sidebottom

The Beginning of Connie & Isaac
Copyright © 2015 D H Sidebottom

This book is a work of fiction and any resemblance to actual places, incidents and persons, living or dead, is purely coincidental.

Copyright © 2015 D H Sidebottom. Please do not copy, alter or redistribute this book.

Excerpts from *The Temptation of Annie* and *My Diary by Mason Fox*, Copyright © 2015 D H Sidebottom.

Please secure author's permission before sharing any extracts of this book.

ISBN - 13: 978 - 1516809134
ISBN - 10: 1516809130

Happiness is a butterfly,
which when pursued,
is always just beyond your
grasp, but which,
if you will sit down quietly,
may alight upon you.

~ Nathaniel Hawthorne.

PART I

Prologue

'In the beginning, nothing but the end greets us.'

Isaac

February 2005. Aged 19.

Pulling my coat farther around me, I turned up the heating dial, shivering against the ice that formed on the inside of the car window, never mind the outside. The music coming from the speakers was quiet and I wanted nothing more than to blast it higher to drown out my thoughts.

I tapped the steering wheel to the beat, shifting my glance to the upstairs window of the house I was watching. Light still glowed from behind the thin curtains, the shadow of a figure moving around behind them.

I needed to wait until they were asleep, to make this easier. For some reason, amongst others, this job felt different. I couldn't put my finger on it. Although the targets didn't sit well with me, it wasn't just that that grieved me. Yet here I sat, waiting to do what I did best.

The shadow in the window appeared to be dancing. I smiled, watching the figure move to what I presumed to be an upbeat tune. The way her hand rested to her mouth, I knew she held a hairbrush, singing for her life.

I grabbed my ringing phone from the passenger seat beside me, rolling my eyes at the number displayed on the screen.

"Yep."

"Hey. You back tonight? The place is flooded with pussy, man. Your father's decided to hold a party for some unknown reason."

I couldn't hold back the growl. I knew the exact reason for his party. "No. I'm out."

"What?" Joel scoffed. "Pussy, Isaac. Lots and lots of glorious pussy. What the hell's wrong with you?"

I rubbed at my face, suddenly tired. My eyes flicked back to the house and I sighed. "I dunno. It's this fucking job. Doesn't feel right."

Joel was silent for a moment. "It's just a job, man. In, kill, out. That's it. That's all it ever is."

"They're thirteen, Joel. I mean, shit. They're kids."

"Since when did you develop a conscience?" he mumbled, but I knew he understood.

"Since I got sent to do the dirty jobs."

"You gonna nail 'em first?"

"What the fuck?" I spat, my lip curling in disgust. "Thirteen, Joel. *Thir-teen*!"

"Fresh pussy." I stared, gobsmacked, at the pattern the ice had formed on the window, tracing the developing web with my gaze as Joel jabbered on. "And hell, if I know girls nowadays, you might not even be their first."

"You sick fuck." I shook my head, wondering what the hell I saw in Joel as a friend. "You're gonna regret saying that when I get back."

"Yeah, yeah. Becca's here," he added, as if to tempt me back.

"Yeah? Go fuck her then. She'll more than oblige." I ended the call, throwing my phone back on the seat.

Glancing back at the house, I murmured a groan when I saw the upper light extinguish. "Fuck!"

I climbed from the car, looking around to make sure I wasn't being watched, and walked around the back of the house. I scaled the high gate and dropped to the ground on the other side, my feet skidding slightly on the frosty ground. My brow quirked at the large fountain standing proud in the centre of the garden, masses of bushes doing half my job for me and blocking me from neighbours' eyes.

My feet dragged along the floor, my heart someplace else. Shit, they were teenage girls. This was never right. What the fuck was my father playing at? I knew he was an evil bastard, but hell, kids? He'd recently started to take kids in, training them into Phantoms, but I'd never been given an order to kill any. And even worse, who the hell had given the order? Which depraved fuck relished in the slaughter of a child?

I traced the length of the wire from the alarm system then slipped the blade from my pocket and severed the line before picking up a stone from beside the door. A key hidden underneath mocked me, making me slightly disappointed with how easy this was. Christ! Did this family have no regard for security? Especially leaving their teenage daughters home alone for the night. Someone, anyone, could break in. I couldn't help the small tilt of my lips at my humour.

It was dark inside, the door leading into a large square kitchen that was only lit by a small ray of moonlight slipping between the blinds. I didn't bother to observe anything; there was no point, and this should be easy enough. I didn't need to be aware of available exits, or objects that may be needed in the loss of my weapons.

I moved silently through the hallway that led off the kitchen then placed a foot on the bottom step to go up to the bedroom. A noise from a slightly open door on the left stilled me, my eyes narrowing and my head tilting as I listened harder.

"I've told you no, Lee. I'm not doing it." Her soft voice seemed to curl inside me. The unique pitch was soothing, even though she sounded frustrated. "She's my sister, and even I'm not that cruel."

I walked silently to the door and pushed it open a little more. She sat on a couch, bent over, painting her toenails a sickly red as she held a phone to her ear. Her long black hair fell in front of her face, hiding me from her view as she slid the brush slowly up each nail, dipping it into the pot occasionally to recoat it.

She giggled into the phone. "No," she breathed, her soft whisper making me wince at how it made me feel. My brow lifted at her obvious flirting. The sound of her laughter made me smile slightly. She was so contrary, flirting one second then giggling like a small child the next. This girl had no idea of the affect she had over boys, but she would find that seduction and teasing are two different things and would one day get her into trouble. Then again, after tonight she'd never… yeah.

"No. Mae's in bed and my parents are in France at some conference of my father's."

I shook my head, pissed off with how her parents had left

them alone at such a young age.

"No, you can't." She gasped. "I'm going to bed now." She sighed and shook her head but smiled to herself. "Goodnight, Lee."

She terminated the call and flung the phone onto the couch beside her. Her head tilted as she studied her toe decorating. "Oh, they'll do," she murmured as her head lifted and she stared towards the TV.

I took a step further into the room, the thick carpet silencing my feet. I frowned when she stilled slightly but she didn't look up. Taking another step, I bit my lower lip when she reached for the phone again, obviously about to make another call. As I reached out to plant my hand over her mouth, she flung herself round and bashed the phone into my face. I was too shocked that she'd realised I was there that it didn't register that she had taken off across the room at speed until she was yanking at some double doors at the rear.

I raced after her and she pulled them open, looking over her shoulder to see where I was. Her bright blue eyes smashed into mine, the terror in them clashing with the adrenaline coursing through her. Her lips were parted, allowing for her deep panting, her chest stuttering as fright quickened her heart rate.

She turned again and disappeared through the doors, bringing us both into a dining room. A huge mahogany table sat in the centre. A large black dresser sat on one wall, plates and glasses perched orderly on each shelf.

My eyes widened when a plate sailed across the room and smashed on the wall beside my head. "Wow." I laughed. "You are a feisty one."

"I'll scream!"

I shrugged. "Go for it. Then we can get your sister down

here and get this over with."

Her head shook rapidly. "No. No, you leave Mae alone."

A glass shattered across my head. Her eyes widened when I growled at her. "Do that again and I will make this really difficult."

"Like it's not already?" She picked up another plate and held it above her head to launch it at me.

She moved around the table when I did, both of us sidestepping, our eyes on each other, our bodies ready to launch at the first opportunity.

"What do you want?" I noticed the trail of tears on her face but her courage surprised me.

"I want you. Simple really."

"W…what do you want to do?"

A small smile crept across my lips. "Well, I'm not going to rape you if that's what you think. Give me some credit."

Her mouth dropped open. "Credit? I… what…?" She stared at me.

"I have standards. You're just a little girl." I smiled at her.

Anger contorted her pretty face as she launched the plate at me. "I'm not a little girl!"

Fuck this. I was tired of playing.

I shot over the table after her. She finally screamed and ran to another door, pulling it frantically.

"Oh dear. Is it locked?" I laughed when I grabbed her, my arms completely wrapping her up. She kicked at me, struggling in my arms as I dragged her across the room. Her head flung backwards, the back of her skull connecting with my nose. Pain exploded in every nerve ending, making my eyes water, and a choked grunt forced up my throat.

"Fuck!" I snarled when I clamped her down harder. "You bitch!"

"Let me go!" she cried, a deep sob wrenching from her as she writhed against me. My chest tightened. Shit, this was so wrong.

Slinging her face down on the couch, I straddled her back, bracing any moving parts as I fought for breath. "Jesus Christ, love. You're a lunatic!"

"GET OFF ME!" she screeched.

"Sshhh." I slapped my hand over her mouth. Her teeth sank into the flesh of my palm. The slap around her head was instinctive as I brought my bitten hand to my mouth, sucking on my own blood. "For fuck's sake, you crazy bitch!"

The heel of her foot thudded into my lower back. I turned around, wondering how the hell she had freed the lower half of her legs. However, I was slightly in awe of her spirit and fight.

I forced her face into the cushion with my hand on the back of her head, and leant into her ear. "Will you stop! I'm seriously considering making your death as painful as possible!"

She froze, her body seizing up beneath me. My heartbeat stuttered. "What?" she whispered, her body now completely lax underneath me.

"It's your time to die, love. I'm sorry."

She was silent, her whole spirit drowned in my declaration. "Why?"

I frowned. I hadn't expected that question. Sometimes kids are more intelligent than the hardest adult who would right now be begging me to let them live, not asking why I was ending their time on earth.

"I have no idea. You're just a job to me."

"How?"

What the fuck was this chick on?

"Uhh, I don't know. How would you like it?" I shook my head in bewilderment.

A small hiccup echoed from her before she tilted her head to the side and looked up at me. Her blue eyes shimmered under the pool of her tears. Her lower lip trembled but she had a resolve about her, a steel spirit that was determined to keep her dignity.

"Please don't hurt Mae," she whispered. "You can do what you want to me, but please, don't hurt my sister."

I stared at her, my heart threatening to break out of my chest. Her eyes locked onto mine as she pleaded with me. My throat constricted, the bile in my stomach threatening to spray across her pale cheeks.

I turned her body under me until she was on her back looking up at me. "Do you know what I am?"

She shook her head, a tear that rolled down the side of her face flinging off and landing on the knee of my jeans. I pressed my finger into it, the damp transferring onto my fingertip. "I'm a Phantom," I told her as I ran the tip of my finger along my bottom lip, tasting the salt in her despair. "I'm trained to kill. I have a contract to end your life."

Her wide eyes stared up at me, her chest heaving as she tried to stop herself from crying. I had never witnessed anyone with as much resilience as this thirteen-year-old girl trapped under my weight.

"I'm afraid that whatever happens tonight, I *have* to kill you and your sister. It's my job."

"No!" She shook her head from side to side, her tears now streaming over her defined cheekbones. "No, please. Leave Mae. Tell whoever sent you that she was in France with my parents. Or... or you could just say that you killed her and they'll never find out. Please! Please! She doesn't deserve this." Obviously she thought that *she* did.

I slid my thumb across her cheek, collecting her tears. She reached down and tore at her t-shirt, ripping it over her head, baring her small breasts sheathed by a simple white bra. "You can take what you want, you can…" She nodded to me, not wanting to voice her words. "Just leave Mae alone."

"Jesus Christ!" I yanked the throw from the back of the couch and covered her with it. "I'm not going to touch you. Not like that."

"Anything," she begged. "Anything."

I looked away, biting down the hatred curling inside me. An idea started to form in my head and I slowly lowered my eyes to her. Cocking my head, I studied her. She was exactly the right material. Strong, feisty, brave, and fucking crazy.

This would cause a shit storm back home, but something told me that it could work.

Pulling in a deep breath I narrowed my eyes on her. "I'm going to try something."

She frowned but gave a slow nod.

I lifted my hand, then paused and lowered it.

Shit!

Lifting it again, I slapped it across her cheek. Her eyes widened as her skin blushed but she bit into her lip, nodding in understanding. She braced herself and turned her face to the back of the sofa. "Do it."

I slapped her again, watching how she reacted to it. After twenty she started flinching, her skin sore, her tears stinging where her skin was starting to break out with tiny blood vessels that had erupted on the surface.

"What's your name?" I asked as I smacked her again.

"C… Connie."

"Connie, listen to me." She nodded, squeezing her eyes

closed as I hit her again. "You're not breathing properly. You're tensing before I even connect with you. Your tears are making this harder. Your fear is making adrenaline which is heightening the pain." She opened her eyes, looking at me curiously. "Breathe in and out slowly." She fought with herself but I waited until she'd taken control, the deep heaves of her chest bating. "Relax your body."

She scoffed at me, looking at me like I'd gone mad. I quirked a brow. She took a deep breath, forcing her body to loosen. I smiled to myself, satisfied with her ability to take orders.

"Now," I whispered as I tilted her to face me with a finger on her sore cheek. "Stop - crying."

She gulped but nodded, calming beneath me. Her compliance made me grin. She scowled at me but I shook my head slowly, tutting at her. She relaxed again, taking another breath, her chest still stuttering slightly.

She blinked when I suddenly struck her twice, once on each cheek. The lift of her brow confirmed that she had followed my instruction perfectly.

"Good." I slid off her. She blinked at me, confused as to why I suddenly relented. "You show promise."

"Promise?"

"Uh-huh." I made my way back to the door and turned. "You will become a Phantom on the night of your fifteenth birthday, in exchange for your sister's life."

Her mouth dropped when realisation hit her, her eyes widening as her breath stuttered. "You're too young now. However, don't think I will forget you, Connie. And don't think you can hide." I smirked at her. "And believe me when I say that no one can get you out of this. Tell anyone and our agreement is void. I will return and I will kill both you and your sister, but next time I won't be lenient." I pulled open the door and looked back. "Do you understand me?"

She nodded slowly.

I winked, clicking my tongue at her. "See you soon."

I couldn't help the large grin from erupting across my face as I left the house. Suddenly, life didn't seem so bad. There was something about the kid that got to me. I had no idea what, but I was sure I would soon find out.

Chapter One

'To prepare for the future, don't think about today.'

Connie

February 2005. Aged 13

THE LUMP OF toast moulded into a ball in my mouth, my throat restricting its passage into my stomach. I still felt nauseous. My eyes were held open by only grit, the lack of sleep making my brain hazy.

"Connie?"

I lifted my head to my father who stood in the doorway with his suitcase in his hand. I quickly flicked my hair so it covered the bruises on my cheek and gave him a forced smile. "You're back early."

He stared at me for ages, his narrowed eyes roaming over my face. "Are you alright?"

My heartbeat increased, my mouth drying further. Could I tell him? He was my father, a cop, and a damn good one at that. He would protect me. However, when Mae's pretty smile filtered into my head, I gulped back the words and nodded. "Yep."

He sighed and lifted a brow. "Then why aren't you at school?"

I frowned at him and looked to the clock. My eyes widened when I realised I was already an hour late for registration. Where had the last two hours gone? "Oh, Lord. I'm sorry."

I shot up, placed my still full mug of tea in the sink, and snatched up my satchel. Father watched me silently, and just as I reached the door, he called to me. "Are you sure you're okay, smudge?"

I winced at his pet name, the name he'd called me since I was two when I painted him pictures consisting of red smudges.

Again, swallowing back the words, I nodded and gave him the best smile I could muster. "Women stuff, Daddy."

He nodded, releasing me from his interrogation. I spun around and smiled to myself. Always worked.

"You suck his cock?" Tammy the school slut asked Bonnie when we were all in the showers after PE. I rolled my eyes when Bonnie nodded quickly. *Lying bitch.*

Mae looked over to me and smirked. I winked, tilted my head back and rinsed the suds from my hair. *His* face emerged in my mind when I closed my eyes, his cruel sneer making my stomach clench, and his vicious words making my eyes sting with the promise of tears. I shivered and snapped them back open just in time to witness a shampoo bottle skimming past my face, the velocity of it making me gasp. I snapped my head round, following its route, and growled when it hit Mae square in the face, her sharp cry triggering another snarl. "Oi, virgin, Mae. It's your birthday next week. Maybe you'll get some cock. Gift wrapped." Everyone laughed. "Then again, I'm sure no lad will manage a hard on with your ugly fucking face."

My blood shifted from my veins into my heart, my anger at their cruel taunts to my sister yet again making me scan the changing rooms for a teacher. Smiling when I found us alone, I leisurely switched off the shower and dragged the towel around my naked body as I scooped up the cheap shower gel the school supplied us with.

Mae blinked, trying to ignore Tammy as she turned her back on the bitch and carried on washing as I lazily walked past her. I kept my face straight forwards as I sauntered past Tammy who now had her face under the torrent of water. Smiling to myself, I squirted a liberal amount of gel onto the floor tiles around her.

As I exited the shower area I couldn't help but grin when I heard Tammy's squeal and then a harsh, hefty thud.

"Take that, you skank!"

I hissed as I ran through the field towards my house, the rain that had come on suddenly drenching me through. I regretted turning down Mae's offer of studying for an hour in the library. Then I rolled my eyes to myself. Why she studied so religiously was beyond me. She was the cleverest girl in the whole school and she was the only student who didn't actually need to study. Me, on the other hand, I was more interested in music, make-up and – Lee. I smiled to myself and re-read his note in my head.

Con,
I can't wait until you see, and feel, what I'm going to GIVE you for your birthday.
L xxx

I knew without a doubt the silly twat thought he was going to get into my knickers at the party. I shook my head and chuckled. It was MY birthday, not his. He was going to be disappointed. No way would I ever let myself be as easy as Tammy. She thought she was clever because she'd lost her virginity, but what she didn't know was what everyone called her behind her back. It frustrated me how all her so-called friends who talked about her slutty ways behind her back would call Mae out for her UN-slutty ways. Two-faced, or what?

I took shelter under a large tree as I looked up at the sky, trying to determine if it was just a quick storm and how soon it would pass. The clouds were black and I knew I was in for a bit of a wait.

A sound from behind me in the mass of other trees caught my attention and I spun round. A scream curled up my throat, and just as it was about to burst from me, he slapped his hand over my mouth. My eyes widened and I shook my head.

"Are you going to be quiet?"

I gulped but nodded, my fear of him making me concede easily. He was tall. I would say early twenties, and his dark blonde hair was long on top but closely cut around his neck. His eyes mesmerised me; their deep green glow utterly stunning. But they belied the evil inside him, the cruel twist of immorality that ran through every single blood vessel within him. He exuded raw power, a malevolence that physically touched me and made every inch of my skin erupt in goose bumps as horror made my heartbeat quicken.

"I didn't tell anyone," I blurted out when he removed his hand.

"I know," he countered softly. For a moment he stared at me with an expression I couldn't decipher. He looked like he was sad but then the glint of his vileness showed me just how dangerous he was. He blew out a breath. "You have got me into some serious trouble, Shadow."

I squinted at him. "Shadow?"

He nodded, his gaze moving over my shoulder. "Mmm, your new name." He brought his eyes back to mine. "Unfortunately my father is…. *troubled* by my decision to leave you and your sister alive."

The way he spat out his father's name made me aware of some issues but it was his other revelation that made the blood in my heart freeze. "What? But you can't go back on it. Please," I begged as I tore off my coat and tie and started to unbutton my school shirt, the rain pouring down on me and soaking me to the skin beneath the thin white cotton. I knew he wanted me, I saw it in his eyes, and if I had to lay flat on my back and let him take what he wanted to save Mae then I'd do it a million times over. "You can take what you want, but please, *please,* don't hurt Mae."

The Beginning of Connie & Isaac

He grumbled at me, his words indecipherable as he took hold of my fingers and stopped me from continuing with my actions. "When will you listen, you defiant girl? I am not going to fuck you. You're thirteen for fuck's sake!"

"But…"

"There's been a change of plan."

I stilled, my mind tormenting me with the options now available. I knew he was going to kill me. I knew it. And when a forbidden tear dropped from my eye, all I could picture was my beautiful sister, her soft smile, her gentle manner, and her strength. I would miss her so much but if this man kept his word then she would most probably be joining me soon. I stared up at him, my body now lax as I accepted my fate. I couldn't overpower him, as hard as I would try. The rain matched the storm in my soul but I nodded. "Please." I slid to my knees before him, my submission making me angry with myself. "Please make it quick, and if possible I would like to go without any pain."

He rolled his eyes and took my hair in his grasp, making me squeal as he yanked me up. "I'm not going to kill you."

"And Mae?"

He shook his head. "If I were you I'd be more bothered about your own wellbeing right now."

"But…"

He sighed again. "My father wishes you to join his family earlier."

I couldn't move. Although I had been terrified of what was to come, I still had the comfort of another year to say my goodbyes to the people I loved. Yet now, everything was being snatched away. "W… what?"

"Mmm," he mumbled with a slow nod. "However." I still remained immobile, the frantic beat of my heart making it difficult to breathe. "I managed to secure you another few months."

I blew out a breath of relief. Thank God!

"Yet we have another problem." I didn't like the way his voice dropped and his tone turned apprehensive. "He's rather... angry. And because I'm his son, he feels the need to make an example of me... and you."

"Me?"

He nodded. "He's going to make your initiation rather... awkward."

"My initiation?" I felt stupid that I was repeating him but I couldn't manage to find my own dialogue.

His eyes narrowed. I blinked in shock and flinched when he lifted his hand and tenderly stroked his fingertip along my cheekbone. My body locked up but my bones felt like jelly, the wobble inside me not matching the rigidity on the outside. His bright green eyes found my blue ones. "There's something about you, Connie Swift, that makes me feel..." He coughed and dropped his hand, the softness in his expression disappearing until a more hardened one overtook him. "You'll need training to be in with a chance of withstanding his torment."

"Training?" There I went again.

He nodded and turned around, his body retreating into the shadows of the woodlands. "Be ready. Midnight, the night of your birthday. I'll come for you." And then he disappeared, my eyes widening when he appeared to just evaporate in front of me.

My heart ached. I ran into the seclusion of the trees and bent, the vomit that surged from me dribbling down my nostrils when my mouth couldn't cope with the fierce reflux.

It seemed that the year I'd had left with my family had

now been cut down to a week. I heaved again when the thought of what was to come fractured my spirit.

Chapter Two

*'When the soul fractures, the heart
holds the pieces together.'*

THE MUSIC HAD stopped. The empty cups and plates were scattered about. Numerous presents were stacked on the sideboard, unopened. Food and drink was crushed into the carpet. All the party guests had gone, and I stood silently staring at my pretty sister, who was asleep on the large sofa in the front room.

Her long black lashes hemmed her cheekbones as her pink, plump lips parted to accommodate her deep breathing. She stirred, mumbling something I couldn't understand as she shifted under the cover I had placed over her tiny body, and turned over, one of her hands tucking under her cheek as she nestled back down.

My parents had booked into a hotel for the night to give us space for our birthday party, and I'd said my goodbye to them hours earlier. Now, as I stared at my sister, my heartbeat became too slow for the rush of blood within my nervous body. I was terrified, horrified to even imagine what was to come. I knew the man wouldn't back down on his word and that he would be here at the stroke of midnight.

I glanced at the clock – five minutes.

I knelt before Mae, tears forming in my eyes as my heart ached and refused to let the words flow. I couldn't say it. I couldn't bid her goodbye. She was my other half, the secondary beat in my chest. Although I'd been a bitch to her on more than a million occasions, I loved her with my entire soul. She was the gentility to my boorishness, the peace to my war, and the conscience to my immorality. But more than that, she was the regular beat in my heart and I knew, the moment I closed the door behind me, that it would never beat properly again.

"I love you so much, Mae," I whispered, tears making my vision blur. "Live life and fall in love. Grant yourself the family you dream of and never, *ever*, give up." I leaned into her, a teardrop falling onto her lips causing her tongue to involuntarily lick it off as I placed my own lips to her forehead. The door opened behind me but I didn't turn. I inhaled her, closing my eyes to etch the smell and feel of her to memory.

A sob choked me and I reined it back. "I give you my strength, sister. I give you my soul and my heart." I stared at her as I stood up, my crying becoming uncontrollable as he stood quietly waiting for me. "But most of all," I whispered. "I give you my life."

I turned and looked at him. His expression was as hard as he was, but sensing my devastation, he lifted his hand to me. I had a feeling it would be the last and only time he would give me any sensitivity. "Time to go, Shadow."

I slipped my hand into his as I picked up my bag with the other and nodded. He led me out but not before allowing me one last look back.

As we silently journeyed farther out of the city and more into the moorlands, minutes turning into hours, my terror and apprehension grew until the rampant, horrific thoughts in my head caused me to turn and look at the dark silhouette of my captor. His cheekbones were defined against the backfill of the moon that bled light through his side of the car. His nose wasn't large as such but, for want of another word to describe it, strong. His lips were thin, the stubble across his chin highlighted in the vague light. He wasn't drop dead gorgeous but there was something handsome and unique about his features. I knew from his accent that he was foreign, maybe Russian or Romanian, yet his English was so good I knew he'd spent more time in Britain than his home country.

Sensing my inspection of him, he turned to glance at me. He didn't speak but his eyes settled on mine as if warning me somehow. I swallowed, and trying to hide my nerves from him, I tipped my head and narrowed my eyes. "I don't even know your name." My voice was quiet and I hated that, but I was amazed I'd been bold enough to ask him.

He turned back to look at the road before answering me. "Isaac Marinov."

The widening of my eyes showed him my surprise that he'd answered. A slow, smug grin stirred his usually stern mouth. "You thought I wouldn't tell you?" I nodded. "It doesn't matter, Shadow. You won't get the chance to tell anyone your abductor's name."

His smart declaration angered me but I wisely held back

the need to tell him that. Instead, I ventured on with my rambling. "Why do you keep calling me Shadow? My name is Connie."

"Not any more, love."

My mouth dried when a sinister smile accompanied his response yet I chose to ignore it. I was scared to death already and if I took note of all his severe expressions and his unkind words then I knew I'd have a heart attack before we reached our destination.

Shifting around in my seat, I blinked at him. "Can I ask you something?"

"Something else?" he mocked, pursing his lips in amusement. Then he sighed and glanced at me again, his stern face even colder than before. "Let me tell you, this will be the single and only time you will ever ask me anything again. You're a Phantom soldier now, Shadow, and I am a Phantom commandant. You do not ask, you follow orders and do them without deliberation, and without disagreement."

I stared at him, my eyes wide. My heart raced at his words. Who the hell was he, and who were these Phantoms he kept talking about? They sounded like an army, or at the very least a clan. I had a feeling I should have allowed him to kill me when he first came for me because I was sure what was to come would be worse than death.

"Speak, Shadow!" he barked, making me jump.

I couldn't form the words when my mouth dried and my throat started to close in. I was going into panic, his cruelness making my stomach heave.

"This is your last chance to ask your question!" he spat. "Don't disrespect my leniency because you won't receive anymore."

I blinked back my tears and jutted my chin out defiantly.

"Who wants to kill me, and why?"

He quirked an eyebrow then laughed. "I did wonder when you would ask me that."

I gritted my teeth, his ridicule making me furious as my emotions shifted gear briskly. I was surprised I'd held it together for so long. "Stop laughing at me!"

I cried out when his fist connected with the side of my face, knocking my head into the window. Amazingly, the car never veered off course, his skill keeping the wheels straight. My hand automatically came up to my sore cheek when pain shot out in all directions from where he'd fractured my cheekbone in one precise blow. My ears hummed and my temple throbbed from where it had thudded against the glass.

"Do – not – ever – talk – to – me – like – that – again!" he stated firmly and slowly through clenched teeth, as if I was too stupid to understand. "The next time you do I will cut out your rancorous tongue and feed it down your throat with my fucking knife!"

I huddled my body into the door, crushing my face into the window and hiding from him and his rage as the tears that had threatened for the past two hours finally came with a torrent of grief and misery. I knew he meant every single word and I contemplated taking him up on his offer just to stop the agony inside my chest from tearing me up slowly and painfully. His way would be a much quicker method of death than the slow death happening inside me.

"Unfortunately, I do not know who gave the order for your death, Shadow," he stated calmly, with a tender smile, as though nothing had happened. It was this coolness and relaxed composure he conveyed that made me aware just how dangerous and malicious he was. Going at lightning speed from violence to softness required an extraordinary control of emotions, and if someone could cause you so much pain then, in a flash, talk to you softly with a gentle smile, I knew they had no soul to give them a conscience. "You will soon learn that Phantom assassins are never given specifics about a mark. Only the basic information."

I blinked, wincing when the action caused my cheek to ache. "Why would I learn that?" I tensed, expecting him to be angry with yet another question, but instead he looked at me with a frown, as though I had just asked the most knowledgeable question.

"Because you'll learn all the guidelines about how you will kill someone."

The nausea that had laid heavy in my gut throughout our journey finally turned into vomit and rushed up my throat at a speed I couldn't hold back from. The few sandwiches I'd eaten at the party hit the dashboard when his meaning reached the part of my brain that understood exactly what he meant – what I was to become.

He tutted and blew out a bored sigh, his disregard to my redecoration of his car making me wonder how many girls had been in this situation. My blood chilled when he spoke again.

"Don't worry, Shadow. Blood and carnage will soon be your drug, the very thing your soul needs to flourish. Your heart will only beat when you watch your prey's stop. And your thirst will only be quenched by death."

I shook my head, shock and horror making it difficult to breathe. "Never," I choked out. "I will never kill anyone."

He laughed. "Sure thing, love."

I screwed up my face and turned back to the window, focussing on the darkness outside before I got myself another punch and retorted angrily to his declaration. I would never kill anyone. Never. I couldn't do that.

Yet, it would only be four months later that I went against everything I swore and promised myself.

At the mere age of fourteen. I, Shadow, assassin for the notorious Phantoms performed my first execution. The first amongst many. The very first one that would split my soul into many pieces, each murder I committed taking away a piece of me until at the tender age of sixteen there was nothing left of Connie Swift but a single sliver of a heart that had always been a part of my sister. And nothing, not even a lifetime of massacre and slaughter would ever take that away.

Chapter Three

*'Facing the future hurts more
than holding on to the past.'*

WE EVENTUALLY PULLED off the road and manoeuvred in between some trees. My eyes widened on a large house looming high and impressive in the background. It was lit by a huge fire on the gravelled area at the front of the house, splitting the darkness in two and giving the house a marbled effect as the heat rose and warped the oxygen in the air.

Isaac pulled to a stop and I remained pressed back against my seat, my heart beating so hard I swore we could both hear its rampant thud in the confines of the quiet car.

"This will be your home for the next three months," he said quietly, his eyes regarding me for my reaction. I refused to give him one. Instead I gulped back the fear and slowly stepped out of the car.

Walking towards the house, I heard Isaac behind me, opening and closing the car doors as he retrieved my bag and followed me up the drive.

The fire was roaring, lighting the area as the house lingered darkly in the backdrop. "Why is there a bonfire?" I asked as I turned to Isaac when he strolled up behind me.

"It's the only heat you'll get. The house has no amenities so you either choose shelter and freeze inside, or take the option of sleeping under the stars with a fire to keep you warm."

My whole body ached at that thought and I instinctively pulled my coat farther around me. Simple things like electricity and gas I had taken advantage of, and now the lack of either seemed daunting. Yet, I nodded, strangely knowing it was expected of me.

Isaac moved from my side and I stared silently at the fire, all the hopes I'd had of my days to come being bearable now turning to ash in the flames of the bonfire.

I frowned when he lifted his arm and threw something into the middle of the raging inferno. I blinked, squinting as I tried to make out what it was. When my brain registered it, I screamed and flung myself forward in attempt to retrieve the item.

Isaac lifted me off the ground with one arm around my body and pulled me back.

"NO!" I screamed as I watched with devastation as my bag rapidly disintegrated before my eyes. "No!" I wrenched free from him as I tried again to take hold of the only thing left of me.

"Shadow!" he roared as he grabbed hold of me again. "Connie Swift is dead! She is no more!"

"But!" I cried, my sobs making my pleas indecipherable, "The only pictures I have of Mae are in there!" I couldn't breathe as I watched my past die. The only physical memories I had disintegrated as fast as my hopes and dreams.

Tears flooded my face as I cried out with a whisper, "Mae. My beautiful Mae."

I fell to my knees, the heat from the roaring fire scorching my skin as I watched everything turn to embers. Rage filled me, my spirit deciding she'd had enough as I bounced up and punched Isaac square in the face, my other hand slapping at him as I made him pay for what he had done.

I was down and under him in a single second. He straddled my back and punched me in the back of the head, pain coursing through my skull with an unbelievable agony. Then he squashed my face into the wet mud until my lungs squealed with the pressure. My eyes began to bulge as my brain throbbed. The world seemed to shift away from me, the hum in my ears disguising Isaac's furious reprimand as the dirt started to seep into my lungs with each of my attempts to draw in air.

Suddenly I was released and the sounds my chest created made me wince as I tried to refill my lungs with much needed oxygen. However, he fisted my hair and dragged me up, the pull on my neck restricting the available passage from my mouth to my lungs, his cruelty once again limiting my supply of air.

"You – ever – strike – me – again!" he hissed, his incense making his pale face turn puce. "And I will end your life! But don't think I will do it swiftly. I will make it as agonising as I possibly can!"

I didn't doubt him for one second. I tried to nod but his hold on my head made it difficult.

"You belong to the Phantoms now, Shadow. You do as you are told, you follow orders, and you do them without deliberation…"

"And without disagreement," I finished in my head.

He dropped me as abruptly as he had seized me. I fell back into the mud on my side, my sobs drenching the already wet ground. I heard his footsteps and then the car door banged. I lay there, in front of the fire, in front of the ashes that were now the only thing left of my sister, as Isaac started the engine and drove off, leaving me alone with only my sanity for company.

Chapter Four

'To fear pain is a burden.
To feed from agony is of profit.'

Isaac

I WAS SURPRISED TO see her still laid out exactly where she had fallen the previous night. I was disappointed, and the small growl that left me told me my soul was too. She had broken already, after a mere few hours. I sighed loudly. She would never have survived my father's cruelty and I supposed it was a good thing she had already given in. A speedy bullet to her head would be the easiest route to give her the peace she craved, yet the gloom inside me irritated me. I couldn't quite figure out what it was about the feisty, mouthy little girl that got to me.

Stepping from the car, the dying heat from the fire prickled against the chill in the early morning winter air, and I zipped up my jacket. Pulling the gun from my waistband I stood over her still form. She really was quite pretty for a stubborn brat, and it was a shame she hadn't proved to be as hard as I originally thought. I'd awoken from a dream in the night, one where she had finally reached the age of consent and I'd given her the best birthday present – my hard cock and the fucking of her life.

Pursing my lips and heaving out another sigh, I clicked off the safety and crouched beside her. Pushing the muzzle into her temple, a sensation in my gut pained me. Why was this so damn hard? I'd executed dozens but I realised I'd never ended the life of a child. Yet, something told me it wasn't that reason that ached me.

My finger pressed against the trigger as a sadness overwhelmed me. Her bright blue eyes were seized by the tiny flames of the fire, unfocussed and unseeing as her fractured mind gave her solace in the depths of insanity. Her lips were tinted a light blue, evidence of hyperthermia rattling her bones and torturing her lungs. The mascara she'd worn for her party left tracks down her face, proof of her tears and the burden of her coherence.

As I hesitated, her eyes slowly and gradually moved to me. "Do it," she croaked.

I blinked, astounded by her lucidity. My head cocked as my eyes narrowed on her. "You still with me, pretty girl?"

She didn't answer but a glint in her eyes showed me enough. I clicked off the safety, stashed the gun back into the waistband of my jeans, and stood up. Her eyes followed me but she made no attempt to move as I walked over to the well and pumped it hard, filling the bucket with ice and the small amount of water that hadn't frozen over with last night's low temperatures.

She shrieked when I poured every single drop over her head. "Get up!"

She cried out, moving quickly to escape another downpour when I hovered the bucket over her. Her head shook manically as her arms instinctively wrapped around her trembling body in attempt to warm herself up. "If you don't get yourself moving you'll freeze to death."

Her eyes widened but the shock of the water rebutted her effort to talk, her teeth chattering so hard she couldn't configure words.

"Run!" I whispered coldly, a wicked smile tilting my lips as I pulled out my blade and flicked it playfully between my fingers.

She swallowed, her feet shuffling backwards as her gawp on the knife showed me her fear.

Lifting it, I aimed it at her then winked. "Run!"

She suddenly moved, her frozen legs struggling with the pace, but I silently admired her strength when she took off like a bullet from a gun, her slight frame moving across the grounds at a speed that surprised me. I gave her a start, needing her to get up a pace that would make her heartbeat increase and pump the frozen blood around her body enough to keep her alive. Then I charged after her.

She looked over her shoulder at me, the terror on her face making me chuckle as she upped her speed and tore off towards the stream that ran adjacent to the three acres of secluded woodland belonging to the Phantoms for both training and executions. Unfortunately, for her, I knew the area well, much of my own training here giving me a blind knowledge of every square inch. She headed towards the stream, and if she didn't brave it and dive in, pushing her aching body through the depths of the freezing water, then she had the choice of facing me instead.

I watched with amusement when her legs slammed to a halt in front of the stream, wondering which option she would choose.

I was slightly awed when she pulled her shoulders back then spun around to face me. She whipped up a long, thick stick from the floor and held it in front of her defensively. Her first lesson was complete and I couldn't help but grin. She would rather brave the worst of the evils, therefore teaching her mind that lighting speed decisions were what would keep her alive.

"Don't come near me!" she hissed, her eyes fixed on the knife in my hand. I was impressed when her concentration never wavered.

"I don't need to," I whispered as I flicked the knife, and she cried out when it embedded into the soft flesh under her right collarbone.

She gasped, one of her hands lifting to the puncture site. "You…"

I laughed. "Don't tell me you expected me to go easy on you?" I tutted as I approached her slowly. "Where would that get you if I make your training easy? You need to see what's to come, Shadow," I murmured as I reached out slowly and took the stick from her, my arms moving quickly to catch her when her legs finally gave in and she fell like a lead weight. I scooped her up and carried her up to the house.

"You know." I sighed as I kicked open the front door and took her into the empty, gloomy room. "I'd have thought you'd have at least attempted to fill the fireplace in here."

She stared at me, her stunned eyes wide from where her face nestled against my chest. "I thought…"

I shook my head disappointedly. "You have a lot to learn." I blinked down at her, hating the sympathy I felt. "You do what is needed to stay alive."

Placing her down on the floor, I went back to the car and

grabbed the stash of medical items I had brought with me. She blinked when I threw them down beside her. "Repair the wound."

Her mouth fell open, her eyes briskly moving from me to where my knife still remained rooted in her shoulder. "What?"

I shrugged. "You either sew yourself up or you will die from the loss of blood."

She flinched when I dipped down, grabbed my knife and pulled it out quickly. She cried out in pain with my brutal extraction, her hand pressing against the wound as she struggled to stem the flow of blood. Her pale face exposed her pain and as I wiped her blood from my blade onto my jeans, I looked at her. "Use that pain and turn it into adrenaline, Shadow. Do what is needed to stay alive."

Then I tossed her the bottle of water I had brought her and left. I wanted to look back, and for some strange reason, it was the hardest thing not to. I never looked back. I never, *ever*, looked back. Yet, before I closed the door behind me, I took a final glance of her. I knew she'd be dead when I returned the next day. She was a tough one, but sadly, she wasn't tough enough to withstand what I had in store for her. And that thought disappointed me and pained my stomach when I slid back into my car and drove away.

Chapter Five

*'Obstacles are not overcome by might,
but by determination and perseverance.'*

Connie

I SENSED HIS SHOCK when he walked into the room and found me eating the berries I'd found growing near the stream that morning. The deep wound in my shoulder was stitched and dressed as a fire roared in the cover of the small fireplace in the room. Fair enough, it had taken me several attempts to fix the gaping slice in my shoulder, and I'll admit, for the first time I appreciated Miss Greer's insistence that I learned sewing at school. The exhilaration that had burst through me when I'd tied off the last of the thread had snapped something inside of me. I can't explain what happened to me in the depths of the dark, cold night. A fever had ravaged my body as I'd sobbed and screamed through every stitch. But when I finally pulled through that last one, and I couldn't help but laugh and cheer myself, it was as though my soul shifted from inside me, an emptiness growing inside me and tearing my heart from my chest in an unbelievable agony that I knew I would never feel again throughout my life. I'd stared at the mess I had made of myself and fell to the floor, weeping, my spirit begging me to end it all as I considered exactly why I had fixed a part of me when I knew death was around the corner anyway. Then I heard her, Mae's soft voice begging me to keep going. I knew it had been my imagination, but it was the slap I'd needed. I was doing this for her, to save her from the hands of these monsters. My death would only negotiate hers. And that was something I was unwilling to spend eternity paying for.

He remained silent, his footsteps growing louder on the cold concrete floor the closer he got to me. Without saying a word, he sat beside me, picked up a berry from where I'd stashed them in a homemade basket made from the cup of my bra, and popped one into his mouth. The small smile on his lips as he stared quietly at the raging fire kept me going for the next three months of his gruelling regime. Whenever I felt the need to give in, I pictured that precise moment, his joy at my resilience and his admiration of my resolve the very thing that made my blood pump harder and gave me the strength I needed to fight back at him.

Don't get me wrong, he wasn't lenient with me. Not – one – bit. His torment and torture threatened to break me, his physical abuse as harsh as his emotional persecution. Before I'd even been initiated into the Phantoms, my body was covered in so many scars that my once thin and weak body was unrecognisable. My abdominal muscles had formed and my tendons were sculpted into weapons and armour. Yet, strangely, I knew he did it to help me, to strengthen my mind and shape my body into a machine for what was to come. I couldn't pinpoint why, and I never asked him, but as I approached the end of my three months trial, spring in the air and warmer nights easing my sentence, our final training session was upon us.

I spun around and flicked my knife, the blade at long last slamming home and puncturing him solidly between his ribs.

"Fuck me!" He laughed then cried out in pain when his knees crunched on the ground as he dropped before me.

I grinned at him, extremely pleased with myself, before I hurried over to the shelf which housed all the medical items and snatched up the needle, thread and some antiseptic. He winced as he pulled himself to the makeshift chair I'd made of sticks, leaves, and old clothing I'd found scattered around the house, then pulled his t-shirt over his head.

I had seen Isaac's body many times during the last three months, and his scars no longer held my attention. It had been the sight of them that had made me swallow back my weakness and strive to be a harder person. If his own father could do that to him, then what the hell he had in store for me was unthinkable.

"Good girl." Isaac grinned with pride as I settled beside him and threaded the needle. He didn't hiss or flinch as I silently sewed up the hole I'd given him. I was always amazed at his ability to push pain aside. As much as he'd tried to teach me how to control pain, it had been the one thing I'd struggled with. Yet, my determination had given me his respect on more than one occasion.

I froze when he softly placed his hand over mine, halting my tending. After three long months of brutal contact, the gentility of his touch shocked me. Not once had he shown me any pity or compassion, and the slight touch was a shock to my system.

I lifted my eyes to his and the pain behind them caused me to blink. Isaac never presented his discomfort to me, and for some reason, I panicked. "Are you okay?" I blurted as I studied the wound in his side. He gently gripped my chin and lifted my face back up until our eyes met again. The pain still shone brightly and I swallowed as my mouth dried. "I'm sorry, I didn't mean to hurt you so much."

He blinked at me and I dropped my eyes to watch his Adam's apple bob. "The pain inside me will forever be irreparable, Shadow."

I didn't know what to say, his openness and soft tone bearing down on me so much that I struggled to breathe. Another emotion flickered across his face and the pain behind his eyes intensified as he leaned to one side and pulled something from his pocket. "I have something for you."

I frowned, unable to see what he held. "What?"

"Tomorrow your initiation into the family will secure your future," he whispered, with so much grief that my stomach clenched with worry. "Connie Swift will be indefinitely erased."

My eyes filled with tears at his declaration. I already knew what he said but his words confirmed it and I couldn't help but grieve for the girl that was once happy and satisfied with the life before her. But she was no more and I verified his statement with a simple nod.

He gave me a nod in reply as he pushed himself up and slipped his t-shirt back over his head. Looking down at me, he blinked softly. "Get some rest tonight. It will be a while before you're granted more."

I nodded again, mutely answering his command. He held out his hand to me and prompted me to take what he offered me. "Guard it with your life, Connie Swift. As of now, you are no longer mine and you'll find that your new master is far crueller and vicious than I could ever be."

As he walked away, I dropped my eyes to the small photograph in my hand, my sister's happy smile beaming back at me. The sob that tore from me caused Isaac to turn back. "Good luck, Shadow. Stay safe and use your head."

And then the Isaac I had come to know walked away, replaced the very next morning by a cold-hearted bastard that would be the cause of many of my nightmares over the next eighteen months.

Chapter Six

'It began with a smile.'

May, 2005. Aged 14.

ISAAC HAD BEEN silent since he'd picked me up. The drive to the Phantom's headquarters was the longest and shortest journey of my life. I could feel Isaac's anguish and that told me that what was coming wouldn't be as easy as the three previous months. I'd thought Isaac was tough, his regime gruelling and brutal, but I wasn't naïve enough to think there wasn't worse to come.

After roughly an hour's drive, we pulled up to some huge black iron gates nestled in the middle of a long, high wall. My heart rate shifted into a higher gear and my brow beaded with sweat. The gate opened. Isaac gave me a sad glance and sighed before he carried on up a mile long driveway, the edges surrounded completely by trees, the woodland seeming to go on for miles.

My eyes widened when a house suddenly came into view, except it wasn't a house. More like a castle. It was utterly stunning. Four ginormous walls of windows and balconies. Isaac drove straight up to some more massive gates bang in the centre of the facing mile long wall, and just as I thought he was going to drive through them, they opened and he pulled the car slowly into an enormous courtyard.

Various people milled about and every single pair of eyes moved our way. The square was enclosed within more walls and windows. The beauty of it took my breath away but a shiver slithered through me when my mind told me that looks can be very deceiving. What, on the outside contained beauty, on the inside held nothing but evil and pain. Isaac was testament to that.

He pulled the car to a stop then climbed out, still silent and brooding. I stared up at him when he opened my door and encouraged me out with a lift of his hand. As I slipped my hand into his, he gulped and gave it a squeeze before the saddest of smiles changed his stern face into an expression of pure agony.

My heart was beating too fast, making me lightheaded, and my belly twisted so much I thought I was going to vomit on the spotlessly clean slabs gracing my way to wherever Isaac led me.

We dipped through an archway, my eyes frantically trying to take everything in as he led me farther and farther into the fortress, because that's exactly what it was; a stronghold to not only keep people out, but also to keep people in.

We walked along endless long corridors, my footsteps silent on the deep pile carpet that shepherded my way into hell. I knew that was exactly where I was going. I could hear it in the silence of Isaac and the pitying looks from the others.

We walked into another long hallway, but this time instead of doors lining the stone walls, this one held windows that displayed another small courtyard. My breath stuttered when I caught sight of the large wooden cross in the middle of it. The grass that had covered the previous larger courtyard had now gone and depths of mud and dirt enfolded the sinister crucifix. However, this one didn't hold Jesus.

"Isaac," I whispered, my voice small as my throat closed up.

He blinked down at me then followed my gaze out of the window. I felt him tense in my hold and I could feel his pulse pumping beneath my fingers. He gulped then carried on, not giving me the soft words of comfort I needed. I stared at him for a moment. Gone was the Isaac I had come to like. His teachings had been rough but he'd also given me privilege to his gentler side on numerous conversations. We would converse easily as we sat roasting rabbits and squirrels around the small fire I would make. Occasionally, he brought alcohol, and more than occasionally, I climbed onto the sheet in the room of the house drunk and giddy. I had enjoyed those moments because they were the things that kept me going. I knew as soon as we entered the Phantom domain that that Isaac had gone for good.

I noticed the people we passed inclined their heads and nodded respectfully at Isaac. Then I remembered he was the son of the head Phantom. I wondered why he had no say over what happened to me if he held that much value in the family. But I was soon to find out that nobody but Frederik Marinov, dictator of the notorious Phantoms, gave orders. And every soldier carried them through, agreeable or not.

Finally we walked through a door which took us into a large room. The people that were chatting suddenly halted and turned our way, their expressions eager and excited. The five people that stood rigidly at the edge of the room turned their eyes to me, but I didn't miss their pitying stares. My body ached under their scrutiny, my heart rampant and giving my blood stream an overload of adrenaline.

Silence descended instantly and at the very top of the room, a tall man, his hair as black as ebony and his gaze just as dark, turned to me. I could sense his powerful aura shift over me, his supremacy making my skin chill with goosebumps.

Isaac dropped my hand and dipped his head respectfully. "Father. Shadow." That was all he said as he backed away and left me standing alone under his father's study. The man was quiet, his head cocked slightly as his narrow eyes slid slowly up and down me. I gulped when he strode across the gap between us and came to a stop before me. He was tall, very tall, and I had to creak my neck to look up at him.

I flinched when his thumb and forefinger gently grasped my chin and he turned my face left and right, observing his new soldier, before a sickly smile covered his face. "So you're the one that cost me so much money."

I frowned, unsure of what he was on about. But I remained silent. My skin was prickling with his authority as his touch turned my blood to ice. But Isaac had taught me well and I allowed him to continue.

"Do you have anything to say about that?"

For a brief moment I was stunned by his question. Then I swallowed against the dryness in my mouth. "I apologise, sir. I'm aware that I am gifted to you in exchange for my sister's life and for that I show my eternal gratitude."

He smirked, his head tipping back as he laughed – at me. But he pursed his lips and nodded. "Your eternal gratitude, huh?"

"Yes, sir."

"Well then, Shadow, let's see how far that appreciation stretches."

I gasped and squealed when he yanked my hair and pulled me across the room. One of the girls standing at the edge of the room winced and dropped her gaze from mine as I looked at her through the blur of my wet eyes. My hand instinctively lifted to his grasp in my hair but as I touched his skin he tightened his hold on me, the pain making my knees buckle until I dropped to the floor. But he continued moving swiftly, dragging me on my knees to a table in the corner.

Manoeuvring me, he slammed my forehead down on the table so I was bent over, and when he pulled my leggings down, I cried out and shook my head. "Please don't!" I sobbed. "Please don't!"

"Father!" I heard Isaac's stern voice behind us. "She's fourteen. She's a child!"

"She is no longer a child, Isaac," Frederik roared back. "She is mine to do with as I wish, fourteen or forty. And I'll demand that you keep your petty whining quiet."

I could hear the hush in the room but I felt Frederik's hand tremble when my bare backside was presented to him. He paused, dragging air through his teeth until the hiss made me shiver. His hand touched the skin of my buttock and a choked sob tore from me.

I gritted my teeth, waiting for it, but when it didn't come I turned to look over my shoulder at Frederik. His gaze held so much hatred and disgust that I couldn't look away. I was caught in the play of his mind, his sick desire racing across his face.

However, he stepped back, his lip curled, before he turned and barked to someone, "Strip her and take her out."

I tensed when I felt hands take hold of my arms and pull me up. "Let's see what you're made of, little girl."

I was dragged back, my feet not touching the floor as two men pulled me through a door and in to the courtyard with the cross I'd seen through the window, sending my terror to a new level. "Oh, God, no!"

They pulled me upright, and through the stream of my tears I saw Isaac leaning on a wall, watching the horror unfold. His eyes found mine, and witnessing my despair, he faintly shook his head at me, telling me in no uncertain terms to suck it up. "Breathe," he mouthed to me. His lesson of breathing through pain seeped into my head and I swallowed back the anguish as I did as he asked and concentrated on filling my lungs to fuel my brain.

I was stripped, my clothes torn from me as one of the men leered at my nudeness. "Shit, it's a shame you're gonna be sore for a while. I'd love to initiate you properly."

"Joel!" Isaac growled. But Joel just laughed and squeezed my boob, giving me a wink when I trembled beneath his rough touch.

Once again, I looked at Isaac. His eyes were low, his gaze on my naked body, but when he lifted them to my face, he winced and turned around then walked away, leaving me with the sick bastards who couldn't help but grope me as they tied me to the wooden cross. I was thankful that they tied both of my ankles together on the bottom, closing my thighs to their wandering hands. My face squashed against the roughness of the wood as my bare backside was shown to everyone in the small yard. Humiliation reddened my face and I squeezed my eyes closed against it. But then, when an excruciating pain tore through my back, they flung open with the force of the scream that burst from me. Another agonising pain sliced through me as Frederik brought the whip back down, his strength scraping my skin from me in the single lash. The scream that left me again made the girl I had seen inside wince for me. My eyes rested on her. She found my gaze with her own and the sorrow on her face held me hostage. When another torrent of lashes belted my back and I couldn't scream for the choked sobs that were suffocating me, the girl mouthed, "Breathe, Shadow." Her chest heaved as though showing me. Isaac's training came to me, and I gritted my teeth but sucked a hefty gulp of air through them, the tremble in my jaw making it difficult. Then when the girl slumped her shoulders, I blew it out noisily. Her chest lifted again, encouraging me, before they dropped and we both blew out together. It didn't stop the pain, but as the torture continued I breathed in and out with the tiny blond girl, her support the only thing that got me through the hour of a torment so unimaginable, my mind zoned out and my brain concentrated on nothing but my breathing and the girl's face.

Eventually, when I passed out, the final thing I saw was her slight nod of her head, urging me to give into the unconscious. And I did it eagerly.

Chapter Seven

'Within the realms of only enemies appears a friend.'

THE BRUTAL AGONY crippling my body forced my eyes open as a choked sob surged up my throat with the vomit.

"It's okay, Shadow. Let it out."

I could barely move but hands directed me over the side of a bed so the flow of sick was guided into a waiting bucket.

"That's it, sister. Let it out." I blinked and frowned at her strange address. I was *not* her sister. The tiny blonde girl who had supported me through the worst lesson of my life smiled softly. "Bullet," she said.

I couldn't answer her for the torrent of abuse my stomach was under, the pain bringing forth a raging illness. My head was sweaty and hot but the rest of my body shivered with a chill. My whole body ached even though it was only my back and backside that had been the focus of Frederik's cruelty.

"And this is Mouse," she added when my gaze swung to the curvy, dark-haired girl sitting on a chair beside my bed. She smiled at me but remained silent.

I gasped when I saw the tube stuck into her arm, her own blood flowing through it and into a drip bag where it then continued its journey through another tube directly into my arm. "What the..?" I spluttered around another round of retches.

"Sshhh," Bullet soothed. "You needed blood fast. You'll get to understand our ways."

I decided to question her about it later. I was amazed and grateful for their compassion and aid but I also wondered why someone hadn't phoned for an ambulance instead. Then I remembered where I was. However, the small square room was new and I blinked at Bullet as I rolled back onto the bed, hissing at the pain in my back before I rolled back onto my side. "Where am I?"

"This is your room, Shadow." She gave me a sad but tender smile. "You're allowed to decorate it as you wish." Her eyes widened and she dragged something from her pocket. "Which reminds me." She handed me the photo of Mae. "This was in the lining of your coat. You were lucky. Just as I was about to incinerate it I caught it sticking out where they'd ripped your clothes."

I snatched it to my chest then smiled at her when I realised how rude I was being. "Thank you."

She nodded and stood up, checking the bag full of blood. "Make sure you hide it from the sentinels. Those bastards will burn it before your very eyes."

My heart sank as everything came back to me.

"I don't think Master likes you," Bullet said with a small laugh as she pulled the needle from Mouse's arm but left me attached to what was left in the bag. "I heard you'd pissed him off before you even got here. Isaac..." She frowned as she studied me. "Isaac went against his own father for you.

Are you two fucking?"

My jaw dropped and I spluttered on my own response. "No!"

She shrugged casually. "Shouldn't be long before you are."

I stared at her with incredulity. What the hell was she on? "I don't think so."

She smirked then shook her head. "Anyway." She smiled as she wrapped her arms around me. "We need to get you up and moving before your wounds set awkwardly."

I cried out when she managed to get me into a sitting position. Mouse appeared with some pills and a glass of water. I smiled up at her. "Thank you." She nodded and smiled in return.

"She can't talk," Bullet said as she gave Mouse a tender touch of the cheek. Her pet name now made sense; quiet as a mouse. Weirdly, Mouse leaned into Bullet's touch intimately. "Frederik cut out her tongue."

My mouth fell open in shock. "Oh my God."

Bullet shrugged. "Don't be shocked, Shadow. Soon, nothing that happens here will shock you anymore." She unhooked me from the drip then dragged my legs off the bed and placed my feet onto the floor as I still stared at Mouse. "Come on," she said firmly. "We need to get you training for your initiation if you're to stand a chance. West need you."

"West?"

She nodded but walked behind me and started to dress my wounds. "Us. West."

"I don't understand." I hissed as she poured a solution down my tender back, but gritted my teeth against the need to cry.

"The Phantom soldiers are split into two groups," she informed me. "The east side of the castle is the East's domain, and they have Joel as their leader. And we take up the west wing. Isaac is our commander."

"*If* I make it?"

She nodded. "You initiation is in three weeks so we need to get you ready. West needs you. East have eight and we're now down to six." Mouse winced and dropped her eyes to the floor before she held out some clothes.

I smiled again as I took them from her but when my gaze dropped to the items in my hands, I spluttered. "I can't wear these!" It was then that I realised Bullet and Mouse wore the exact same items of clothing. The black leather leggings and tight black leather top made my heart beat quicker.

"Why?"

"Well they're… they're leather – and tight."

Mouse rolled her eyes then waved a hand over the front of her body, showing me that she also wore it, and maybe it didn't look so bad.

"It's either wear what they give us or walk around naked. And let me tell you, it's fucking hard enough keeping the sentinels' hands away from you as it is." Bullet sighed and moved around to the front of me, kneeling down and looking up at me with pity. "Shadow, your old life is exactly that. Old. Now you need to adjust if you stand any chance of surviving, and you need to do it quickly, sister."

I stared at her then swallowed. "My initiation?"

"That will be announced during supper," she said as she helped me into the clothes, my body twitching in pain as the material grazed over the burning welts. "It's always Master's instruction but you will go up against the new East probationer."

My mouth dried as I slipped my arm through the armholes in the t-shirt. "And what is usual for initiations?"

Bullet shrugged as she dragged a brush through my long black matted hair and tied it in a bunch behind my head. "Sometimes it's a simple fight. Sometimes it's a 'who shoots who first'…" My eyes widened more and more at her revelations. "…and sometimes it's a case of who wants to go to hell first."

My heart rate was going crazy, my blood chilling when I started to understand what she meant. "Am I expected to…?"

"Kill?" She finished for me when I couldn't say the word. I nodded. "Yep."

That was all she said as she took my hand and led me from the room.

We emerged in a huge room after twenty minutes walking through the castle into the south quarter. Long wooden tables topped with cutlery and condiments were lined up side by side, some of the seats taken and some empty. A large table ran horizontal to the others along the top of the room and my eyes found Isaac's where he sat beside his father at the centre of it. An expression I hadn't seen in him before covered his face when his eyes slowly dragged down the length of me. His lips parted and his tongue came out to wet his lips. I shivered. I'd seen lust before but never really in Isaac's expressions. I'd caught him looking at me from time to time, but the way he looked at me now was completely different, apart from when he had observed me naked on the cross.

"Come," Bullet said as she took my hand and led me to the far left table. Numerous people looked up and gave me smiles and welcoming words. "This is Panther," Bullet announced as she directed me into a spare seat opposite a tall man with long, thick brown hair as she and Mouse sandwiched me protectively between them.

Panther grinned and leaned across the table, shoving his hand out eagerly. "Welcome to West."

"Thank you," I replied quietly.

"And this is Rogue." Panther presented the guy to his left as he poured me a cup of water and placed it before me after filling his own. I smiled at Rogue. His eyes twinkled at me, his ebony hair tied behind his head. He was good-looking and I chastised myself for thinking so at the most inappropriate time.

"Hi," Rogue said; his smile was soft and real. "You look like a tough one. Just what we need." His gaze roamed over me as he spoke, his stunning blue eyes fixing on my torso held in the tightness of the black leather. "Hopefully we have someone who can finally get through the initiation."

I swallowed my nerves as a string of people dressed in black filled our table with plates of food. "I'll do my best."

Every person at the table dived into the mass of food. The three meats and copious amount of vegetables made my stomach growl appreciatively, and I leaned forward to scoop a small portion onto my plate.

"You'll need to do more than your best," Rogue continued. "You'll need to give your life to the exercise." He regarded me, the question in his eyes of whether or not I understood.

I nodded, dropping my eyes from his intense stare. "Bullet's filled me in."

"You need more food than that," Panther said. "It could be a while before we get fed again."

I frowned at him as I shovelled some mash potato into my mouth. The first properly cooked meal I'd had in three months was nectar to my hunger. "What?"

He piled his own plate high. "Master decides if we are to be fed or not."

I stilled with my fork halfway to my mouth. "What?"

Rogue rolled his eyes as Panther sighed. "Shadow, right?" I nodded. "Shadow," he paused and blew out a breath. "What Master says, goes. What Isaac, our commandant, says goes. What the sentinels say, goes. Us, soldiers, have no say in what happens. Until you make it to sentinel, then I'm afraid you have to suck it up and take what is given when you can."

"Before we make it to sentinel?"

Rogue nodded, piling more food onto his now empty plate. "Assassins for the family are called sentinels."

"Then I'll never become a sentinel!"

He chuckled and shook his head. "Gorgeous, you'll become whatever they want you to become."

"But," I grumbled, ignoring his term of endearment. "I won't ever kill anyone."

All four of my new friends chuckled but when a whistle resounded from the top table, they immediately downed their cutlery and stood up. Bullet dragged me up by my arm. "Stand firm and still," she whispered. I noticed her instant stiffness, her chest sticking out as she looked over to the head table.

"Good evening, Phantoms." Frederik addressed the room as he also stood. "We have business to attend to." He gave two men who stood by the table a nod. They took the arms of a man and dragged him to Frederik. Frederik narrowed his eyes on the man and curled his lip in disgust as he tipped his head menacingly. "It seems you failed to carry through with your designated contract."

The man whimpered, struggling in the hold of the two men, but they were strong bastards, their muscles huge and their faces marred and ugly, giving them a threatening appearance. "I'm sorry, Master!" the man quickly spoke.

Frederik pursed his lips and nodded with the same expression he had given me when I had declared my gratitude to him. A chill raced over me and I shivered against it. My eyes sought Isaac's once more and found that his own pure green irises were fixed on me. He blinked and quickly turned his focus back to the man in front of Frederik. "You know the rules, Vex."

The man, Vex, shook his head manically. "Please, Master, I beg of you. Give me another chance to prove my loyalty to you."

Without another word, Frederik turned and picked up a knife, then swiftly slid it across Vex's throat.

A scream burst into the silence of the room and it was only when every head turned my way that I realised it had come from me. Frederik's eyes narrowed on me. "Ah, yes. The second matter of the night." I stared ahead, not really hearing or seeing anything as my focus remained on the man who was bleeding out and twitching on the floor.

"Drag it in, Shadow!" Bullet hissed quietly.

"Both probationers approach the table."

Bullet nudged me and I blinked at her, the haze in my head breaking. She nudged her chin towards Frederik. "Go on."

I looked around the room and found I was the attention of every single eye. Gulping, I slowly made my way to the front. I refused to look at the dying man and my gaze found Isaac again, but this time he was looking anywhere but at me. Frederik's eyes were narrow on Isaac as though waiting for him to look at me.

When I approached the top of the room, a huge, dark-skinned boy came to stand beside me. He looked as terrified as me, the whites of his eyes yellow as he physically shook before me. I attempted a smile but he quickly looked away. I frowned, wondering what had crawled up his arse.

Frederik smiled. "Look at you both!" he said with a delightful glint in his eye. "This one will be fun. I think you deserve something... special."

I stiffened when I caught Isaac wince, his teeth gnawing on his bottom lip, but he kept his gaze trained on his father.

The boy beside me made a funny noise and glared at me through the corner of his eye. What the fuck had I done?

"Shadow seems like she'll be a fun one to go against, Ice." Frederik laughed when Ice, the boy beside me, tensed. "So let's make this interesting. Three weeks from now, the twelve of June, both of you will go against each other in Bleak Woods."

A range of gasps rang out and I frowned at Isaac when his horrified eyes flew to me. I tensed when the shock the room displayed told me my initiation wasn't going to be as straightforward as usual.

Frederik smiled at me, the hidden message in his eyes not lost. "May the strongest be brought back before me."

Isaac was still staring at me with wide eyes but when Frederik turned back to him and coughed, Isaac blinked and turned his pale face to his father. "Seems you have your work cut out for you, Isaac." He laughed then turned to Joel, who I only just noticed was standing beside Ice. "As do you, Joel."

Joel grinned but Isaac remained quiet and sombre. However, they both nodded their understanding.

"Continue!" he barked, and the room burst back into activity.

Bullet stared at me when I retook my seat between her and Mouse. Panther and Rogue looked at me sadly. I picked up a bread roll and pulled off a piece, forcing myself to eat although my stomach twisted anxiously. "I take it Bleak Woods isn't much fun."

They all remained mute but Rogue shook his head. "No one ever goes out into those woods. Ever. What the hell have you done to piss him off?"

"Rogue!" Isaac barked behind me, making me jump. I looked up at him as he snapped his eyes to me. "Come with me!"

My friends lowered their eyes and continued with their meal as I shifted out from the bench and followed Isaac through the castle and into the west wing.

Isaac's hand felt warm against the coolness of my clammy skin. My brow dripped with sweat and my rosy cheeks showed my fever, but the ice that ran through my veins with what had just transpired caused me to cling to Isaac harder. My eyes saw Vex dying, and his body jerking as his heart came to a stop, but my mind played over the scenarios concerning my initiation and what hell I was to face. He tolerated my firm hold for the route through the castle but when he pulled me through a door at the north side of the west wing, a room of massive proportions opening up to us, he swiftly dropped it and raked his fingers through his thick hair.

"Fuck!" he hissed as he paced across the room, leaving me staring at him nervously. He muttered quietly under his breath as he poured two tumblers of whiskey and passed one to me.

His eyes finally landed on me and the depths of his green eyes bored through me. His stare was so penetrating that I didn't dare move or break away from it. His lips parted the way they had in the dining room as his eyes slid down the length of me.

An angry sneer travelled across his face as his chest heaved. "Why are you fourteen?" His bizarre question was quiet and I wondered if he'd meant to speak it out loud.

I frowned. "I'm sorry, I don't…"

"Fuck!" He shook his head firmly. "You look like edible sin dressed in that. I need my cock sucking!"

My eyes widened and I gasped, bringing his eyes back to my face. He shook his head and his own eyes widened. "Fuck, Shadow, I didn't mean you. I'm not a baby bouncer…" My eyes widened farther with each of his words. "Fuck!" he murmured before he downed his alcohol and went to refill his glass. "Sit down!" he barked. I wasn't sure if he was angry with me or himself.

Eventually, after he drew in a long breath, he came to sit in the chair opposite me in front of the large roaring fire. The room was, as were most in the castle, like something from the period dramas my mother loved to watch on TV. The walls were all stone, as was the floor. The furniture was almost regal, and definitely luxurious, unlike my own barren room that held a bed and set of drawers. Yet every mod con and gadget available to man was scattered around the room, taking away from the majestic feel. A huge stereo and TV sat to one end of the room and an up-to-the-minute PC sat on a chic glass desk to another side. Huge heavy curtains covered the windows but the walls displayed a vast array of modern art. The whole feel of it made my head spin with the many clashes to the eyes and mind.

Isaac rested his head back on the chair and sighed, his tiredness clear in every action of his body. When he remained silent for a long time, making me wonder why he'd brought me there, I bit the bullet and surged ahead.

"I take it Bleak Woods lives up its name."

He blew out the breath he'd just inhaled and opened his eyes. He let his gaze settle on the ceiling. "No. To live up to its name it should be called 'Death Woods'." My heart shuddered. He really wasn't helping to put me at ease.

My mouth dried and I nodded slowly. "Right."

He growled then sat up and looked at me. "The woods are untouched by anyone. The bogs there take hostage of even the hardened hunter. The trees are so thick and dense that they give no respite, instead tangling you in their branches until you slowly die." My heart struggled with the manic beat, my pulse racing, but my fear slowed its frantic pace until I felt dizzy with the conflicting emotions. "The environment itself eats the fucking wildlife like the place is frozen in prehistoric times." He shook his head again but dragged a breath through his clenched teeth. "However, we're lucky it's late spring. That gives you a longer period of light," he rambled more to himself as his eyes became distant and he stared at the fire. "But your hunting skills are already good so that gives us time to concentrate on your fighting skills."

I took a large mouthful of the whiskey and gulped against its roar in my throat. It settled into my belly where it bubbled with my nerves. "Isaac," I whispered, but he didn't appear to hear me.

"Rogue is an ace at stealth. He would be good to train you up for all covert moves." He nodded more firmly.

"Isaac," I repeated, my voice choked as I struggled not to let the despair swallow me.

"Although I've taught you well with a blade, your sniper capability could be enhanced, that way you can take him out from a distance should the chance arise."

He finally looked at me when a choked sob tore from me. I'd tried to hold it in but the more he rambled on, the more the despair had clawed its way out. I shook my head, the tears tearing down my face as furious as the rush of blood through my system. "I can't kill him. I can't kill Ice. I can't kill anyone!"

For the briefest moment, his eyes softened and the sorrow reflected back at me made my weeping harden. But then an austerity took over him. I gasped when his hand struck my face. "You can. You have to. Don't you dare give in now. I, for one, will not allow it. You're mine, Shadow, and both I and West need another soldier." His face was red with rage as I held my throbbing cheek and sobbed. He gripped my upper arms and shook me. "You are a Phantom! Control your damn babying."

I hiccupped, trying desperately to drag my emotions back, but that just made a weird sound break from my chest. Isaac shook his head. "I'm not listening to your whining. Fuck off. FUCK OFF OUT OF MY SIGHT!"

I stared wide-eyed at his cruel disregard. Where had the Isaac I knew gone? Although he'd been strict with me before, he'd still been compassionate and patient. His relentless teaching had been accompanied with a sympathetic encouragement. But now that was gone, and all that remained was a harsh hunger for me to give his 'regiment' another warrior. It had all been a ploy, his compassion a way to make me fight for his team, a way to butter me up so I would give his unit a better chance against the other side. Well fuck him. Fuck him to hell.

Pulling my shoulders back, I swallowed hard and stood up. "I will do my best, for you, because I know how much this obviously means to you," I grated out with a coldness that made him still. "But to be quite frank, I don't care, and I know you definitely don't, if I don't come out of those damn woods."

With that, I turned on my heel and fled his room.

Chapter Eight

'Prepare for the worst. Fight for the better.'

June, 2005. Aged 14.

IT WAS THE night before the initiation. Frederik, or Master nas I'd come to call him, had thrown a huge party. I'd thought it rather sick, but as the alcohol started to flow, easing my nerves and worries, I'd started to see it as a good idea. Definitely a good idea when Ice collapsed towards the end, his alcohol consumption so high he'd drunk himself, and his worries, into obliteration.

Fall Out Boy's *The Phoenix* blasted through the speakers just as Bullet forced another beer into my hand. "Come on, Shadow." She pulled me across to the space cleared for a dance floor, both of us thrusting our bottles into Panther's hands as we weaved through the mass of other dancers into the centre.

"I'm gonna change you like a remix," Bullet belted out of her drunken mouth as she pointed to me. "Then I'm gonna raise you like a penis!"

I laughed loudly, shaking my head at her adaptation of the lyrics. She grinned back at me as she placed her hands on my hips and turned me around so she could grind against me. "That's better. Smile. Forget tomorrow for an hour and live. It could be your last party, sister."

I closed my eyes to take in her words, but when I opened them, my body went stiff. Isaac was drinking in the middle of a few sentinels. My stomach clenched at how handsome he looked in tight black jeans and his customary boots. A simple grey t-shirt hugged his muscles. I frowned and peered closer, wondering what it was about him that looked different, until I realised his blond hair had been dyed black. However, it wasn't him that grabbed my attention, it was the tall blonde, lithe girl, hanging on his every word that made something strange happen to my insides. She giggled at something he said, and he turned to look at her and smiled back. Just as I was about to close my eyes and cut them out, he leaned into her and kissed her.

Bullet, sensing my sudden change, rested her chin on my shoulder and looked to see what had captured me. She sighed before she spun me around to face her. Her eyes were narrow and probing. "Please don't tell me you feel something for Isaac."

I shook my head, but the blush that heated my cheeks outed my lie.

She closed her eyes for a second and dragged in a breath. "Bloody hell, Shadow. You can't go there. For one, he's our commandant, and for two, Isaac doesn't do relationships. He fucks. That's it."

I lowered my eyes. I had been telling myself the very same thing for the last three weeks. Yet, I had caught him looking at me slyly, a distant look in his eye and a longing on his face. Once or twice, during the times we had trained alone, I knew he had come close to kissing me but he'd backed off, mumbling something about my age.

Bullet grabbed my arms, her grip fierce as she shook me. "Shadow. Isaac is a mean bastard. He is known for fucking you once then turning his back on you. You think that screwing him will give you a better chance in here?"

My mouth fell open at her accusation. "What? No!"

Mouse had come to join us and her eyes were wide when she figured out what we were talking about. Bullet glanced at her then a cruel smirk contorted her pretty face. "Mouse will tell you!"

I stared from Mouse to Bullet, trying to tell myself that she didn't mean what she had insinuated. But when Mouse blushed and looked away, my jealousy over the blonde bitch with Isaac was nothing compared to how I felt towards Mouse.

Bullet made me look at her again, but this time the sadness that covered her face brought tears to my eyes. "Isaac will never love you, Shadow. I'm sorry I sound so cruel but you need to learn what he's like. He'll fuck you, most definitely, but he will never hold any feelings towards you. Ever."

Her blunt words hit me hard. Taking another look towards Isaac I found him in the blonde's embrace, his mouth moving hungrily on hers. He opened his eyes and caught me looking. His brow furrowed before he pulled away from her. She stared at him quizzically before she followed his line of sight. Her eyes narrowed on me before a cruel smile filtered across her face.

"Who's that?" I asked Rogue when he meandered over to us.

He looked across and I didn't miss the way his body stiffened when his eyes found the object of my question. "Fuck!" he hissed. "What the hell is she doing back?"

Panther huffed. "Finished her latest assignment in record time apparently."

"Who is she?" I asked again, my mouth moving but my gaze fixed on Isaac while he stared me out.

"Becca." Rogue grated out the name with a tone full of hatred. "She's one of the assassins. She's been in France on a contract."

Mouse shook her head at me furiously, her hand sliding across her throat. It was a warning. And one I took heed of if my friends felt the need to alert me.

Rogue looked between Isaac and me, his eyes hard. Suddenly, he slid his arm around my shoulder and turned me around. As I looked at him to question what he was doing, he pushed his mouth to mine and started kissing me. I was so surprised, I couldn't do anything other than stand there like a lemon and let him kiss me. A range of whoops and whistles rang out, but just as quick as he'd kissed me, he drew back. It was only when I saw Rogue's shocked expression that I realised Isaac had pulled him back.

We all stared at Isaac as he glared at Rogue. My heart panicked but I remained silent. I knew Rogue was in trouble and I desperately wanted to ease the shifting rage between the pair.

"He was just wishing me good luck for tomorrow," I said lamely.

Isaac moved his glare to me. "Really?" We stood rigidly, waiting for our leader to bark an order but when he did, the others frowned and I gawped. "Meet me in my quarters, Shadow." When I stood still he growled angrily. "NOW!"

I nodded then scurried off, but not before I heard him spit

at Rogue. "Have you touched her?"

My heart beat furiously as I stood in the middle of Isaac's living quarters. I couldn't understand what had just happened. My mind contemplated different scenarios as to why he'd pulled Rogue away but I couldn't find an answer for any of them.

When his door flew open, I stepped back at the anger he radiated. He fixed his eyes on me then slowly stalked towards me. I knew I was in trouble but I couldn't figure out why.

As he advanced I stepped back, moving away from his fury, but when my back hit a wall and I couldn't move, I had no choice but to stare him out.

"How much have you had to drink?" he barked.

I shook my head in confusion. "Uh, about three bottles."

He scrutinised me deeply, his gaze boring into my soul. "Are you sure? Are you drunk?"

"No!" I shook my head furiously. "No, I'm not drunk. It's the initiation tomorrow. I'm not that stupid!"

"Aren't you?" he whispered, his voice a mere breath. "You seem to be."

"I don't understand." And I didn't. I'd limited my supply of alcohol. I'd trained hard and religiously over the previous three weeks, sometimes falling in bed at three a.m. to be up again at six, so his anger with me was uncalled for.

I gasped when, with lightning speed, his hand grasped my chin and he yanked my face to his. "Has Rogue taken your virginity?"

My eyes were as wide as my mouth. "What? Of course not! Of course he hasn't!"

He chewed on his bottom lip like a maniac, his teeth scraping the thin layer of skin from it. His chest heaved with his rage but there was something in his eyes that called to me; a need, a longing, a softness he only ever showed to me.

Before I could question his strange expression, his mouth descended on mine, the warmth of his broken lips scraping at my own. I gasped into his mouth but that seemed to only empower him. My back pressed against the wall as Isaac pressed against me, his tongue probing and seeking entry. I tried to stop him, my fists bunching the material of his shirt in my hands but I was powerless, and if I was honest, I was as much his puppet as he was my master.

He groaned when I let go of his shirt and lifted my hands to his neck, clasping them around him and pulling him to me. The heat from his kiss was intoxicating, his greed making my belly throb with a warmth I had never experienced before and his reverence making me kiss him back just as hard.

He pulled away and sighed, resting his forehead against mine. "You have no idea how much I want to be inside you, Shadow. To feel your heat on me." He groaned to himself as he closed his eyes. "On your sixteenth birthday, your virginity is mine."

I gawped at him, shocked but amazed by his declaration. Yet I knew what he said was the truth. I hadn't been wrong about him, I had seen it in him. "It's yours," I whispered, making his eyes snap back open. But I swallowed. "That's if I come back from those woods tomorrow."

He was silent for a moment, pain pouring from him as he looked at me. Lifting his hand, he softly cupped my cheek.

"You will. You have to. You're mine, Shadow. And not even death will take you from me."

Chapter Nine

'In the depths of hell, we find ourselves.'

I FACED THE CLUSTER of trees at the south entrance to Bleak Woods, the shadows they set on the ground around my feet a warning of how I was about to be eaten in their depths.

My team, West, were silent in the seconds before I ventured in. I could feel their despair and terror for me. Each one settled their hand on my shoulder, giving me a squeeze of comfort before they filtered away, leaving me with Isaac.

I heard his heavy swallow and turned to him, forcing a small smile. "I promise."

He gave me a nod, his gaze locking me in his spell as he reached out and grabbed my hand. "You do what you must in there, Shadow. For the first couple of miles you'll be safe… well, from Ice, anyway. He's coming in from the north entrance so it'll be a good way in before you meet him." I nodded firmly. "Use whatever you can, and take what the woods give you naturally."

I nodded again, desperately trying to moisten my dry

mouth. "Is there a time limit?"

He shook his head. "No. You need to come back to the south exit though; that's the only rule. Whoever exits from their respective entry point wins. If you leave from the north, you lose."

"But I thought it was just the one out that wins."

"Well, it is, but if you fail to leave through this point you'll still lose. That's all there is to it, really. Kill Ice then come back here."

"So simple," I whispered as I squeezed my eyes closed.

Isaac clenched my hand hard. "You can do this, Shadow. I know you can. I wouldn't have insisted you were on my team if I didn't think…"

"You requested me?"

"I did. So don't let me down, pretty girl."

His eyes softened on me for a moment. He turned to look over his shoulder, searching for the others, but when he found them further down near the bottom of the hill, he leaned forward and pressed his lips to mine. "I'll await your return. Stay safe and use your head, my love." He turned abruptly and walked away, leaving my heart spinning with his endearment.

Blowing out a breath, I turned back to the woods. Looking down at the shadows around me, I smiled. The shadows were on my side, their worship of their namesake giving me their strength. "Let's do this," I whispered to them as I ventured in.

Every creak, every whispered sound, caught my attention and I spun in circles for the first hour until I forced my heart rate to settle. I chastised myself. My nerves were my enemy and unless I got a grip of myself then I knew I would lose. I'd thought every noise was Ice, that he'd found me and I was about to kiss my life goodbye.

The density of the trees was like a manmade trap. Every now and again their gnarled and jagged branches tore at my skin, their roots causing me to stumble in the darkness of its depths. Leaves, weeds and undergrowth had me hissing curse words more than I managed to gain farther access into the forest. My body shook with a chill after I'd had to crawl through and over some streams, the bottom anything but smooth as sharp rocks and stones ripped into the bottom of my boots. The trees kept out any natural light so my clothes remained wet and heavy against my icy skin.

Stumbling through to a small clearing, I blew out my breath and plonked down onto the ground as I reached into my backpack for some water. Taking a gulp, I noticed a high and rounded pile of leaves and debris, obviously made from some sort of wildlife. Clambering across to it, making sure there were no baby animals nestling inside, a faint smile curved my lips as a plan came into my head.

Snatching up a stone and some more dry branches, I rubbed at them furiously like Isaac had taught me, a small cry of glee leaving me when some sparks leapt out and started to kindle the arid leaves. Blowing gently on it, I clapped my hands, proud of myself when the debris burst into small flames, each licking its kindling and burning harder and harder until, as I built it up, it burnt savagely.

Making use of the fire, I winced as I burnt the leeches from my body, their teeth retracting sharply as I took the small torch to their ugly, slick bodies. "Get the fuck off, you little bastards. I need my blood, thank you."

My body ached, my muscles screaming in pain now that I had started to relax slightly. Isaac and the others had been right. Bleak woods had proved to be more torturous – probably - than the upcoming fight with Ice. I hissed when I applied some ointment Isaac had given me to the Cuckoo Pint's stings and then stabbed myself in the leg with a prefilled syringe to counteract any spider bites I'd taken on my way through the dense foliage without realising.

All I wanted to do was sleep, to curl up beside the fire and rest but I knew if I wanted to live, I had to stay on my guard.

So, when the smoke started to billow up and rise through the high trees, I scurried backwards and hid in the shadows, waiting for my opponent to show himself.

It wasn't too long before I heard branches snapping, and a rustling from the other side of the clearing. My heart was threatening to give me a coronary and I blew out a freezing breath as quietly as I could. Slipping my sniper rifle from my bag, I settled it on my shoulder and looked through the sight, moving it quickly left and right as I searched for Ice. Sweat beaded my brow even though the cold ravaged my veins. My head pounded as my anxiety spiked. Licking my dry lips, I whispered to myself when the leaves of a bush moved. "You can do this, Shadow. He's your nemesis. He will kill you if you don't kill him. You need to live. For Mae. For Mae."

As soon as I saw his dark hand slowly push back a branch to take a look, I fired, ignoring the pain in my heart. I hissed when the bullet embedded itself in the tree beside his head. "Fuck!"

A bullet whizzed past my own head as I ran on bent knees back to another tree.

"Shit, shit, shit," I murmured when another round of bullets tore through the air, one of them flicking my hair with its closeness.

He was getting closer, his bravery outweighing mine as he ran towards me. My heart stopped beating as I wrestled with one of the gnarly roots that had trapped my foot and sent me flying forwards, my rifle sailing through the air and thudding against a tree at least ten feet away. Time seemed to stop as I rolled onto my back and stared into the barrel of Ice's rifle.

For a long moment, neither of us spoke. A loud hush sucked at the atmosphere around us, even the slight rustle of the trees stilling as we linked our eyes and communicated within the silence. I could hear his heartbeat as though it was my own, the pure ache on his face reflecting my own, and the shame and guilt he battled with matching my own. But then he spoke. "I'm so sorry, Shadow."

I sucked on my lips to stop the sob from bursting from me. Yet, I smiled. "I know. I know." My vision blurred and I blew out a breath, then nodded. "Make sure you exit north, Ice."

He frowned at me. "What? Why?"

"Did Joel not tell you? You need to exit from your own entry point."

He looked stunned by my help but then sniffed and nodded as his own eyes welled up. "Thank you."

Tears filled my eyes and I swallowed. "Just do it. Get it over with."

He hesitated and squeezed his eyes closed as I knew he would. Hating myself, I took the opportunity and kicked out at his gun, sending it flying across the air into the direction of my own. Before he could comprehend what was happening, I jumped up and sprang at him, taking us both to the floor. His head hit a rock and he cried out but his strength was astounding. He clamped his legs around me and rolled us until I was under him. "You bitch!" he hissed as he hit me over and over, my eye swelling immediately as my cheekbone cracked. His large hand pressed around my neck, his fingers squeezing. My brain swelled with the pressure, my eyes bulging as my pulse raced into dangerous territory. But still he squeezed, his lips curled back and his teeth bared as he took my life in his hands and forced my lungs to contract with the sudden absence of air.

My fingers clawed into the depths of the earth as I frantically tried to dig a way out. But there was no way out. Ice was stronger than me. I had been a fool to think I could take him on. Isaac had warned me of his strength, and had told me to use my wits and strength to take him out. And I had tried. I'd used the fire as a distraction, but that single bullet had failed me. I knew Ice deserved to win. He'd make a much better assassin than I ever would.

Yet, just as the world started to leave me and my body started to float, Isaac's words whispered through my head. *'You're mine, Shadow. And not even death will take you from me.'*

Like God was for once looking down on me, my fingers clawed at something hard. The stone Ice had hit his head on. The stone that already held my rival's blood. But as my fingers curled around it and I stared up at Ice, the choice of finally putting this nightmare behind me snapped into my head and I hesitated.

Did I want to be eternally owned by The Phantoms?

If I won this, what would become of me?

Did I forever want to owe them my life to save my sister's?

Should I infinitely put my fate in Frederik's hands when his hatred for me was so evident?

Would I just be better off allowing Ice to send me to a better place, a place that finally promised me peace?

And as I looked up to the clouds, I made my decision.

Chapter Ten

'Never lose hope. But be careful what you wish for.'

Isaac

I CLENCHED MY JAW hard and looked up to the darkening sky. She'd been in there too long. Much too long.

"Ten hours and twenty seven minutes," Panther said quietly, his own face lifting to the sky. "If she's not out soon, she'll be in there for the night, and quite frankly, I don't fancy her chances much then."

Rogue blew out a noisy breath beside me, his face towards the woods as it had been for the past ten hours. I knew he held feelings for Shadow and I was angry with myself for becoming emotionally involved in their relationship. Shadow had sworn, as had Rogue, that there was nothing between them, yet the way Rogue had behaved this last few hours, I was sure he would have liked it if there was something there.

"You're quiet," I said as I turned to a silent Bullet. Her eyes flicked my way, her face full of concern and sadness. "What are you thinking?"

She sighed then shook her head. I was stunned to witness tears in her eyes. Bullet was a tough cookie, her resilience as strong as her aim, and she'd become one of my best, yet her lack of confidence in Shadow angered me.

"She'll be back!" I snapped as I turned and walked towards the edge of the forest.

My eyes peered ahead, my focus trying to shift past the bulk of the trunks and branches, but it was a hopeless task, the growth so thick my eyes couldn't get past the first cluster of vegetation.

"Where are you, pretty girl? Where the fuck are you?"

A spot of rain landed on my head, and once again I looked up as if I expected the skies to give me some clue as to what was going on in there. I was positive my instincts hadn't been wrong about the girl. She was tough and she was clever, but there was a part of me that knew she prayed for the end. Who didn't in this fucking place? We all did in some way or another. My father was a tyrant, the fiercest and most dangerous of all my kin, but one day, I knew... I knew I would end his rule... and his life.

A noise straight ahead caught my attention. For the briefest moment I couldn't inhale a breath. My heart hung heavy with hope, my eyes flicking left and right along the stretch of trees as I tried to pinpoint the sound. However, when a rabbit leapt out, I hissed and aimed my gun at it, blowing it to pieces in anger like it was its fault he didn't bring Shadow with him.

"Bloody hell!" Rogue puffed out as he ran up to me. "I thought it was her then." I nodded, gritting my teeth.

Bullet walked over to the bunny and started to chuckle, her merriment soon turning to a laugh. We all turned slowly to her. She was bent over, hysterics evident as tears ran down her face.

"What the fuck?" Panther asked.

She turned to us all, her face alight with happiness and humour. "She made it!" She laughed. "She only fucking made it."

We all stared at her as she lifted a strand of cloth. "It was tied around Roger the Rabbit." She laughed so loudly I thought she'd lost it, her face red and her eyes glowing.

She stumbled over to me and held the piece of cloth out. I quirked my eye at her as a small smile lifted my lips before the biggest grin I'd ever held covered my face.

"What the hell is going on?" Rogue barked as he moved his eyes from a hysterical Bullet to me.

I winked at him and held up the scrap of white cotton, probably what was left of Ice's clothes. 'I'm hungry, get me on the barbie,' was emblazoned across it in what looked like charcoal.

"Well, fuck me!" Panther gasped when out of the thickness of the trees stumbled the most beautiful sight in the whole damn fucking world.

Shadow. My pretty girl.

Chapter Eleven

*'We may win the fight but the battle
becomes all the more arduous.'*

Connie

THE MUSIC WAS loud, and the alcohol once more flowing. Lush foods piled high on the table as all of West celebrated my win. The two remaining West soldiers, Woods and Tank, who had been on an assignment in Germany with two of the assassins, had returned, welcomed me to the fold and joined in the revelry.

Isaac, who had pulled me into the bathroom and kissed me like his life depended on it, had scurried away twenty minutes ago after mumbling something under his breath about his cock being hard enough to hammer the nails in his own coffin, and Mouse had applauded my victory by lovingly decorating my room with soft pink walls and fancy lights around the ceiling, her own stash of cash paying for my luxuries. She had been delighted when she'd witnessed my happy tears with her amazing makeover and I'd pulled her into a massive hug, her thoughtfulness drowning my jealousy over what had happened between her and Isaac. All in all, everyone was joyful. Everyone except me.

My mind whirled at what I had become. A killer. I stared at them all partying hard, their drunken dancing making my heart ache. To them it was a normal day, and victory was more important than someone's life.

Rogue, spotting me in the corner, smiled at me sadly then came to sit beside me and handed me a tumbler of hard liquor. "It does get easier."

I blinked, taking a large mouthful of the scorching liquid but needing its burn to calm the chill in my body. "How?"

He shrugged. "I don't know." He sighed and placed his hand on my knee, giving it a slight squeeze. "But it does."

I looked at him, a deep frown on my face. "How long have you been here?"

He blew out a noisy breath, his lips rattling as he contemplated my question. "God, about six years now."

My eyes widened on him. "But you must only be around seventeen."

He nodded, unconcerned by my shock. "My father sold me to Frederik when I was eleven." I stared open-mouthed at him, my face displaying every single bit of my disgust and disbelief. Smiling, he placed a finger under my chin and gently pushed my mouth closed. "Careful," he whispered. "Keep your mouth open too long round here and a sentinel will be popping something in there that you really don't want."

My mouth fell open again as my eyes bulged, but when he winked cheekily I couldn't help but giggle.

Woods, his nickname given for reasons I won't repeat to you, grinned lazily at me when The Black Keys *Lonely Boy* came on the stereo. He swung his hips playfully to the sixties track as he danced over to me, a mischievous glint in his eye as he crooked his finger at me. I didn't miss how Rogue's body tensed beside me, but when Woods took my hand and yanked me up, slamming my body against his, I once again found myself laughing at his wicked play. "Dance with me, Shadow. I have four weeks of getting to know you to catch up on. You're the *it* girl now. Everyone wants a piece."

He grabbed my hand and twirled me, spinning me out before he pulled me back to him. He sang to me, each word accompanied with a huge toothy grin. His long blond fringe moved as eagerly as he did, and before long, every single West soldier was up and moving as one as Woods taught us the dance moves to the song. We looked like something from *Fame* as we spun and skipped across the stone floor in the communal area of the west wing, our heavy stomps echoing around the stark hallways.

We all came to a halt when Frederik walked into the room. The smile on his face made me shiver. "Are you having fun?"

We stilled, the music still playing loudly until Mouse slithered over to the stereo and turned it off, the silence suddenly deafening.

"Oh, don't stop on my account," Frederik continued before he swung his gaze to me. "I've just come to borrow Shadow." My pulse was racing because of the dancing but it bottomed out when he narrowed his eyes on me. "Walk with me."

Before waiting for me to acknowledge his order, he turned around and walked back out. All my friends winced, giving me worried glances. Bullet grabbed my hand as I walked past her on my way out. "Don't let him bring you down, sister."

I gave her a nod and hurried to catch up with my master.

He glanced down at me. "I must say, I'm surprised and quite delighted in your victory."

I blinked, nearly voicing an "Oh" before I caught myself and managed to be diplomatic as expected. "Thank you, Master."

"I honestly expected you to fail, and that Ice would be another triumph for East." We carried on through the west wing, passing my own room and making me wonder where we were going. "It seems my son has seen some potential in you that I neglected to see."

I frowned when we came to a stop outside Isaac's quarters, and Frederik turned to me. "I must ask, though… have you instigated a relationship?" He asked the question softly, as though his calm voice would force an admission from me.

I shook my head but I knew from the way my body stiffened that he'd caught my anxiousness. He drew in a breath, a faint growl signalling his annoyance. He smiled then opened Isaac's door and gestured for me to enter.

I swallowed heavily then stepped inside, my heart beating wildly. I was terrified for Isaac. Even though he was Frederik's son I knew it wouldn't stop him punishing Isaac if he had found out how we'd become close.

What I didn't expect was for my eyes to find Isaac standing in the middle of his room, his jeans around his ankles, and Becca knelt before him frantically sucking his cock as his fingers twisted harshly in her hair.

My whole body heated with a flush, and a deep sorrow settled in the pit of my stomach. My heartbeat pounded in my ears as my skin crawled. I couldn't move, shock freezing every part of me. Isaac's eyes found mine then flicked to his father before he pushed Becca away.

"Oh, please continue." Frederik smirked. His tone and

lack of surprise told me he knew exactly what was happening in here, and his reason for bringing me suddenly hit me. I stumbled back a little but when Frederik gripped my arm and yanked me forwards. I winced and tried to look away.

"I – said – continue!" he barked to a stunned Isaac and Becca.

Isaac stared at me almost sorrowfully, his staring eyes slowly blinking but Becca gleefully grinned, her eyes mocking me as she dipped forwards and took Isaac's hard dick between her lips. Isaac gritted his teeth and closed his eyes, shutting me out as Becca sucked, her noisy slurps bringing forth a sharp gasp from Isaac before she moved back and let him come all over her bare breasts. At fourteen, I had never seen a penis before, and after witnessing the man I'd fallen in love with with his down another girl's throat, I swore I never wanted to see one again.

"You may leave us now, Becca," Frederik announced.

She frowned but nodded and picked up her t-shirt, smirking at me as she passed. I diverted my eyes, not giving her the satisfaction of seeing the dejection in my eyes.

"Can I help you, Father?" Isaac virtually spat as he pulled up his jeans and zipped them up.

"Hmm." Frederik nodded. "Seems as though you two have developed a close relationship. I have an assignment for the pair of you."

Isaac's brows knitted together. "What?"

Frederik pulled two brown envelopes from his jacket pocket and thrust one at Isaac and one at me. "Yes. I think Shadow needs to see how you work, Isaac. After all, the girl seems totally taken with you. Perhaps this will be fun for you both."

"But she's just a soldier," Isaac protested. "I'll take a sentinel."

Frederik growled and stepped up to his son, his rage potent as his chest heaved. "You'll do as you are ordered!"

Isaac pulled in a breath, his jaw clenching with his own fury, but he nodded. "Of course."

"You will leave tomorrow. Everything is ready for you." Then he turned to me, a cruel smile on his face. "I think you'll enjoy this one." He walked away, but when he reached the door he turned back. "Oh, and Shadow, just because you're leaving the Phantom headquarters doesn't mean you can... go on an adventure alone. I know exactly where Mae lives."

My eyes widened and my mouth dried. I gave him a furious nod, telling him I wouldn't flee Isaac, even if the chance arose. I would never risk Mae's life. I was there for her, after all.

"Good girl." He chuckled. "Well, have fun."

When he disappeared, I turned to leave. "Shadow!" Isaac called out, but I carried on walking, ignoring him.

Catching up with me quickly, he grabbed my hand and dragged me into the kitchen, slamming the door closed behind him to block out his father who was still strolling down the corridor.

"Get off me!" I hissed when he took my hand.

"You shouldn't have seen that," he mumbled as he dragged his hands through his hair. "The bastard!"

"Who?" I scoffed. "You or Master?"

He glared at me. "Don't be pissed at me, Shadow. It was just a blowjob!"

I froze, staring at him like he'd just grown another head. "Just a blowjob?" I choked out with incredulity. "Just – a – blowjob?" I pushed at him, my hands slapping at his chest.

He snatched both of my wrists into one of his large hands

and pushed me, the base of my spine pressing into the long metal preparation table. "Be careful, pretty girl. Be very careful."

"You bastard!" I shouted as I struggled with him, but when he slapped me hard across my already bruised cheek, a strangled sob ripped from me, the last twelve hours finally bursting from me in a torrent of emotional despair. "I killed him for you!" I cried out. "I bashed his head in with a fucking rock until my face was covered with his brain and his blood. I had to gamble on not being frozen to death in the damn stream just to wash it from me. I did it for you! I did it all for you! And you... you repay me by..." I screamed again. "Just leave me alone. I wish I had let Ice fucking kill me! I saw my life in the end of his gun. It was pressing into my head." I snatched my hand from his and poked my finger into the centre of my forehead. "Right there. Right. There. He aimed his fucking rifle at me and told me how sorry he was."

My fists punched at him, my tears rolling off my chin in an outpour of grief that tore my soul out with them. He grabbed me by the shoulders and pulled me to him, his quiet shushes making me hate him more, every single one of his fake words of comfort driving a stake through my heart.

"Get off me!" I spat as I pulled away.

He glared at me, his fierce stare displaying all of his anger. "It was just sex, Shadow. Sex. You seem to be confusing sex with sentiment. Fucking, screwing, oral or even a finger in your arse. It's just sex. A primitive action of enjoyment. Why are you so hurt by it? We've only kissed for fuck's sake!"

I shook my head sadly when he rolled his eyes and leaned back on the counter as he opened his brown envelope. He obviously thought I was a silly girl, a girl who couldn't control her emotions. But what he forgot was that I had been thrust into adulthood four months ago, the night he decided to use me to anger his father. Because I was sure that's all I was; an act of rebellion, a "fuck you" to his father's tyranny.

"Forget it," I whispered as I turned and started to leave.

"Shadow!" Even through my anger and rage, even through the deathly hum of grief in my ears and the incessant humming in my head, I heard his chilling tone. His face had turned grey as his once fierce green eyes turned to a drab colourless mass. He stared at me with wide eyes, his mouth open as if trying to say something, but his shock leaving him stunned and mute.

Frowning, I pulled out my own instructions.

I had to read the target's name three times before Isaac raced across the room and caught me.

Mark: Graham Anthony Swift

My father.

Chapter Twelve

'Envy, sorrow and fury, a heady combination.'

Isaac

SHE WAS QUIET beside me throughout our journey, her face to the window or her head back and her eyes closed every time I glanced her way. I knew she was still pissed with me. I sighed in irritation for the millionth time. I should never have grown as close to her as I did. She didn't understand how things worked, how sex was just a release, and in a way that was my fault; she was just a kid after all, and I'd failed to explain how things were between us. Yes, she'd had to grow up quickly in the previous four months but still, what the hell did she expect me to do, struggle with blue balls for the next eighteen months? Yeah, not a chance.

"I wish you would tell me what you're thinking," I said gently, my pussying around her angering me, but I was desperate for some conversation. Since she'd seen her father's name on the paper, she hadn't uttered one word. When I'd fetched her from her room at 5a.m. that morning, she had been sitting, ready and waiting on her bed with a determination that, quite frankly, worried me. She wasn't allowing herself to be honest and accepting, and that gave way for trouble. I couldn't afford for her to get sentimental during the job or this could go horrifically wrong.

She glanced at me but remained silent. She needed to find some strength or this was going to be a disaster. Going against all I had told myself through our journey, I reached under my seat and pulled out the other brown envelope, the printout of what Devlin, my secondary in West, had been feverishly working on overnight for me. Devlin was a Godsend, least of all because his latest screw was the secondary to Joel, and Devlin had been craftily fucking all of East's secrets out of the stupid bitch. I couldn't fault him, really. A good shag and inside information; he was a sly fucker. But luckily, a sly fucker who showed me his loyalty over and over again.

She frowned but took the papers from me. My stomach lurched but I hoped it did what was needed. My mouth dried as she slowly pulled them from the envelope and started reading. I couldn't understand my reactions to her. I had never before cared about any fucker, especially a woman, but every single time I was near her my cock was hard and my heart was soft. Fucking hell. I was screwed.

I sighed again at my own thoughts but Shadow must have thought it was in sympathy for her because her first gasp and the way she looked at me with tears in her eyes made my fucking stomach vault.

"Keep reading," I commanded, trying to be hard because pity and softness were the last things she needed.

"I don't understand," she said quietly as I pulled onto the

street of her former home and parked a few doors away. A shiver trapped me in a moment of viciousness when I realised exactly four months ago I had parked in the very same spot and changed Shadow's future, and not for the better. And now she sat beside me a killer, a Phantom.

"He... my Daddy is... a human trafficker." She shook her head, denying what was written in front of her.

"Well, technically, he's a slave auctioneer. But yeah, he's a trafficker."

I couldn't help but pity her. My father was no better than hers but I had grown up knowing exactly what he was. Shadow had had a childhood, a happy one, but to find out it had all been a lie, and the parent you loved and looked up to was just a lowlife prick must have been shattering.

"Since I was three," she mumbled. Her head shook slightly as she carried on reading, her eyes furiously moving across the four sheets of paper as she meticulously read every single word.

She finally lifted her gaze, her eyes unfocussed as they looked to the greying clouds above us. "I always wondered how they could afford such luxuries on a cop's wage." She sighed. "Yet my mother has no idea."

"Apparently," I mumbled in reply as I squinted at a figure walking up the road. Her head was down as she dragged her body along. But it was her long black hair shielding her face that caused my heart to stutter and the pit of my stomach to growl nervously. *Shit. Fucking shit!* Stealthily, I hit the door lock button with my elbow.

"Thirty eight girls. Thirty - eight - fucking - girls. How the fuck...? What kind of... evil, vile, twisted bastard..." A growl resonated from her and I stared at her in surprise. I had expected her to deny it, or at the very least have a fucking breakdown, but instead she seemed to change before my very eyes. Her body stiffened, and her chest heaved with each of her deep pulls of air. Her eyes glazed over and her jaw clenched. Her bright blue eyes transformed to icy grey as a malevolence seeped from her.

Then she spotted her. Mae.

A strange long whimper rang out in the quietness of the car. I thought she'd try to get to her, but instead her hand clawed at me, desperate for my own hand as her sweaty palm sought mine. I grabbed her hand and held it tightly, trying to give her comfort and strength as she started to weep.

"Oh… I…" Her head shook as tears scurried down her cheeks. "My beautiful sister," she cried out with a deep wail. "Isaac… I… Mae… Mae…" she whispered randomly, unable to put together words in her grief.

"She's doing okay," I whispered back as I leaned forward and softly kissed her forehead, once again hating that I needed to soothe her distress. This girl was going to be my death warrant.

She looked at me, and for the first time ever my heart clenched with hatred for not only my father, but for myself. Shadow, out of everything, missed her twin like someone had cut her in half, which theoretically, they had. "You've been watching her?"

"Well, not really but I've made sure I've been up-to-date with her life." Catching her chin in my thumb and forefinger, I directed her sad gaze to me. I needed her to shift back to a Phantom, and quickly, when I saw her father's car crawl up the road towards us. "Your father is the reason you now belong to Frederik."

She froze, her eyes narrowing, and the hatred that fuelled her stare made my heart beat a little quicker. "What do you mean?"

Sighing, I blew out a long breath. "He owed money. Lots and lots of money. To my father. You and your sister were to be killed in debt of that. But because I... didn't follow that through and took you, saving Mae, my father now calls for your father's death."

We weren't ever given details of a kill, but I'd managed to piece together certain things, and after Devlin had done his work it had all come together.

Slowly, she turned her head and watched her father pull into his driveway. She watched in silence when he climbed from his car and smiled towards Mae who slowly walked up the drive. He said something to her and she shook her head, her sad gaze shifting to the ground. I'd seen the flyers and the desperate television appeals they had done when Shadow had left with me, and I knew that Mae was the backbone of those appeals. It was like her father really wasn't bothered. He'd carried on doing business as usual. The heartless bastard. Her mother had gone off the rails slightly, from what I'd managed to find out. She'd started to drink heavily and would take off for days at a time. But then again, I supposed the family home was no longer a close family unit since Shadow had gone. I blinked to myself, wondering how much pain a parent went through. I supposed the not knowing was the hardest thing. I made a mental note to finalise their grief for Shadow's sake.

Graham slid his arm around Mae's shoulder and pulled her to his chest, consoling her when it was obvious she was upset.

Another snarl tore from Shadow. "How dare he touch her? How dare he taint her in his sickness!"

I couldn't help but slyly smile. She was like a hungry dog

with the scent of a rabbit. The energy and loathing emanating from her made me euphoric. It seemed all my hard work had finally trickled into her soul.

Three hours later, when darkness descended and the house lights extinguished, I turned to Shadow who hummed vigorously beside me. "Are you ready to do this?"

She chuckled and the sound made my skin freeze. "Oh yeah." She nodded slowly as her teeth clenched with hatred. "Oh yes."

Giving her a nod and praying, I released the door locks. She dipped for the small black bag beneath her seat, tore the balaclava over her head and stepped from the car.

Pulling my own headpiece down, I climbed out of the car and ran behind her as she rushed across the road. She scoffed when she entered the key code for the large gates. "Stupid bastard should have changed them," she whispered.

I didn't reply. Instead I allowed her precedence. She needed to lead this and for the one and only time, I would be her second.

She ran around the edge of the bordering wall and ducked beside his car, then without waiting for me to do or say anything, she climbed underneath. Her hand appeared from underneath and I handed her the cutters. Within seconds she had cut his brake cable and slid back out.

We ran back down the driveway, and as we reached the gates, she turned around. Sadness poured from her. I could physically feel her sorrow as she stared up at one of the bedroom windows. "Goodnight, my beautiful Mae," she whispered. "I love you. Be happy."

Then she turned back round, gave me a firm nod, and we left.

And she never returned.

Chapter Thirteen

'Life for necessity.'

Connie

"HARDER." PANTHER SAID as I punched the bag again. "Use your knuckles, not your fingers." The bag swung further when I twisted my hand a little, doing as he instructed and connecting the leather with each bulging knuckle. He smiled and nodded as he caught the bag when it spun towards him. "That's it. Better."

I'd been grateful when Devlin had announced it was a training day. The thoughts of what I'd done two days ago to my own father were torturing me and I was hungry for a diversion. Although I had been eager for his death after I found out what he really was, nightmares of his death being slow and painful had tormented me. After all, he was still my father, even if he was an evil fucker. But knocking the shit out of a punch bag had been a Godsend and kept me sane.

Sweat ran down the centre of my nose and dripped from my chin, mixing with the damp patch on my t-shirt. My muscles burned after two whole hours of training and when Devlin nodded at us both, I grabbed my knees and attempted to regulate my breathing. "Much better, Shadow."

"I'm starving," I groaned when my belly growled. Apparently, Frederik was in one of his moods and breakfast had been 'cancelled'. Luckily, Mouse had been saving snacks, hiding them in her massive cleavage to sneak them out and had built a small stash, so she'd handed Bullet and me a couple of biscuits around eleven that morning before training started.

"Supper's up in thirty," Panther called over his shoulder as he grabbed his towel and rubbed it across the back of his neck. "Although, looking at those hips, you could do with a salad."

"You cheeky arsehole!" I chuckled and flung a bottle of water across the room at him when he winked cheekily.

Devlin laughed at our antics and I smiled at him. Devlin was okay. He was strict and harsh with our training but he was also considerate of our situation. I'd heard Joel was a bastard to East, and I was relieved we had Isaac and Devlin on side. I hadn't seen Isaac since we returned after our first assignment together, and I had to admit I was somewhat upset by his lack of support. I was sure he thought killing your own father wasn't a big deal and that made me wonder what sort of monster he really was.

We all stilled when the door to the training room swung open and Frederik appeared, regarding us all with an inquisitive stare. I could never quite determine where his mood was at by just looking at him. His face was always impassive but there was something in his eyes when he turned them on me that made my body freeze. Slowly he walked farther into the room, Panther and Devlin watching him carefully as his fluid gait brought him closer to me.

He clicked his tongue and sighed. "I always knew you'd be a disobedient bitch."

I blinked, my brow creasing in confusion. "I'm sorry, Master?"

His eyes blazed with anger and I couldn't seem to breathe properly.

"We have strict rules here, Shadow. And you seem unable to follow them." I gulped when two of Frederik's sentinels entered the room. "But you will."

He twisted and nodded at the two men who walked over to me and took hold of my arms, their grip fierce as their fingers dug into my flesh.

"Master?" Devlin questioned, his eyes rapidly flicking from Frederik to me, his own bewilderment as visible as my own.

"Your commandant and your soldier are being disciplined, Devlin. It isn't hard to understand. And if you value your position in this family then you will refrain from contesting my decisions."

Devlin shook his head. "I'm not questioning…"

"They both fucked up an assignment!" Frederik spat, his lip curling with distaste. "You should be grateful, Devlin. Isaac's incompetence has temporarily awarded you his position."

Devlin's eyes widened in shock as both Panther and Devlin looked at me in surprise, like it was my fault that Isaac had been reprimanded for something I wasn't aware of. My heart hammered in my chest. Isaac and I had followed the order, we'd completed the assignment given, so why were we being punished?

"I don't understand." My head shook as Gregory and

Jacob dragged me across the room but they stopped when Frederik lifted a hand.

"You were given specific instructions, Shadow. An easy target."

I nodded, trying desperately to defend myself. "And we carried them out. I, myself, cut the cable on my father's car."

He chuckled, the chilling sound making my skin crawl with anxiety. "And did you hang about to see the job through?" When I gawped at him his hand snatched out and he seized my face in his fingers, his grip bruising and painful. "No, you didn't. You failed, Shadow."

I choked back a gasp. "You mean I didn't kill him?"

His anger was stifling me but his strong hold was not nearly as agonising as his next words. "Oh, you killed him. But you also killed your mother."

Nothing registered after that. My heart tore into so many pieces that I could feel the blood seep into my soul, tainting it with the evil force that lived inside me. My body moved but my mind couldn't shift from the horror imprisoning it. *I had killed my own mother. I had killed my mother.*

A visceral scream broke from me as I sagged in Gregory and Jacob's hold, their hands the only thing keeping me upright as they pulled me through the mansion. People stopped and watched us, some pitying, some appalled. My own corruption blinded me, the smothering reality of my mistake fracturing my sanity until nothing but bleakness tinted my vision.

Why was life so cruel? What had I done to warrant such a sickening existence? I'd followed fate's orders, accepted what it had given me, but time and time again it had proved cruel and persecuting.

I had orphaned my sister. My actions had left Mae alone.

I didn't even recognise that I had been stripped and tied to the cross. My sanity had left me; I was numb and broken. My body became an open invitation for the many Phantoms to act out their sick desires on but I didn't care. What they did to me I still cannot remember to this very day. My mind left me for so long that when Bullet and Rogue gently lifted me down five days later, I didn't know who I was.

Nothing of Connie Swift remained; her skeleton housed Shadow's emotions and thoughts. My body was more than just damaged and abused in those long and lonely days; my spirit was destroyed beyond any hope of repair.

I would never be the same again. It didn't matter what happened next because I didn't care. I wanted to die. I wanted the heavens to accept me but I knew God would never accommodate my sins. And if it wasn't for Frederik's promise to take Mae in lieu of my death then I would have taken a knife to my heart long before my soul froze with hatred.

I never saw Isaac after that day. He had been sent away by his father for his part in my parents' death, and I realised when Frederik's cruel words taunted me, that mine and Isaac's closeness had deepened his hatred for Isaac. It hadn't been Isaac's fault. I was to blame for it all, but Frederik wouldn't accept my apology. He wanted to make an example out of both of us, and he did so every day in Isaac's absence until nothing he did surprised me anymore. Pain became welcome because it was the only thing I actually felt. My skin bore the story of my life, the many scars and traumas the only proof that I lived; everything on the inside was dead and empty. The flowing of my blood was the only escape for all the abhorrence I stored up, yet simultaneously the brutal force of my hatred was the only thing that made my heart beat.

By the time Isaac returned two years later, I was such a different girl. The Phantoms had finally managed to do what they set out to… destroy Connie Swift and replace her with a cold, merciless killer.

Part II

Chapter Fourteen

'We bleed to breathe. And we bleed together.'

Connie

November 2007. Aged 16.

GUY RIVERS LOOKED like Ian Somerhalder and had the personality of a llama with a belly ache. He was the proprietor of Rivers Casinos, a chain of entertainment clubs across Europe. He also, as I'd found out over the previous four hours, liked the sound of his own voice and had a nervous habit of scraping back his inky black hair from his oddly large forehead. Sweat beaded his brow whenever he got animated in his story telling, and I noticed the more gin he drank, the more redder his lips became.

"...And I said to Brian, 'When you have as much money as I have, you can smile at yourself like I do every morning.'"

I forced a smile and fluttered my lashes. "And do you?" I was bored and needed to get the egotistical prick into his hotel room.

He peered at me like I'd just spewed random French at him. "Do I what?"

Cocking my head a touch to the side, I ran my tongue across my lips. He swallowed heavily when, gently, I sank my teeth into my lower lip. "Have lots of money?"

His chest puffed out and I only just managed to hold back a roll of my eyes. "I have a filthy amount, Rhianna."

Bringing my wine glass to my mouth, I blinked slowly and gazed at him. "Do you know how wet that makes me?"

A slow grin crept across his handsome face. "Sometimes, just to remind myself of how rich I really am..." He leaned towards me and I held back a shiver when he trailed his fingers up my arm and lowered his voice. "...I masturbate on the bed covered in twenty pound notes and shoot my load right across her majesty's pretty little smirk."

I sank my teeth into my tongue in attempt to stop the bark of laughter from escaping. What an utter fucking dick. "I think I would prefer you to shoot your load across my face."

He spluttered on the mouthful of gin he'd just guzzled, his eyes forming wide circles, but when he puffed out a hot breath I knew I had him. "I have a room here."

"You do?" Of course he did; did he think I didn't know that?

He nodded slowly, his eyes dropping to my chest. "It has a very comfortable bed."

Shrugging casually, I pursed my lips. "Who needs comfy beds? I'd rather you bent me over a couch and fucked me hard and fast."

I thought he was going to have a coronary when his face turned puce and a vein throbbed in his temple, his lips parted, and he started to pant like a damn dog. He snapped his fingers at a passing waiter. "Bill. Now!"

"Certainly, sir."

The waiter reappeared almost instantly and Guy thrust his credit card at him. "Hurry up!" he snapped.

Holding on to an irritated sigh, I smiled at the waiter and fished a twenty out of my purse when it was obvious my date wasn't going to tip. "Thank you, your service has been impeccable."

He grinned at me gratefully. "Thank you Ma'am." He gave Guy a short nod then smiled at me again before he left to cater to another couple on the next table.

Guy stood as I pushed back my chair and rose. His pale green eyes were hungry as they slid down the length of me then came back to my face. He pressed a hand to the base of my spine and guided me to the elevator in the foyer, once or twice his palm lowering until it skimmed across my arse.

Sometimes, like then, I wondered why, but Mae's pretty face smiled in my mind and I released a sad sigh. Guy, hearing me, ran his finger along the length of my jaw. "I'll make you feel good, Rhianna."

Chuckling quietly, I nodded. "Oh, I know you will."

His chest puffed out as his pride swelled and I glanced at my watch, annoyed at how long the bloody elevator was taking to climb all of five floors. It was Mouse's birthday and I was eager to get back for the party. "This is us," he declared excitedly when a ping heralded our floor and the doors opened.

His room was a cheap, basic one which genuinely shocked me. I'd have thought this egotistical prick would only go for the more luxurious suite. He wasn't short of a bob or two. The one hundred thousand pounds transferred into the veiled Phantom bank account from his own that morning was testimony to that.

As though better than me, he stood staring at me in the middle of the room, waiting for me to worship his dick. Clicking my tongue at his obvious self-worth, I slid my dress up over my hips, showcasing my black thigh high boots and bare pussy. "Get on your knees and lick my cunt."

His mouth popped open at my order, his brows shooting into his hairline. I smirked when he visibly shivered, his lust overriding his system. Following my demand, he walked over to me then slowly lowered himself down in front of me. His eyes snapped to the junction of my thighs as he lifted his hands and pulled my flesh apart with his thumbs.

As soon as his tongue delicately touched my swollen clit, I sank my fingers into his hair and pushed his face further into me, encouraging the boring twat to get a shift on. I didn't have all night and I had work to do, an orgasm was just an added bonus.

He mumbled something but took the hint and started to work me faster. Arousal slicked his tongue as he circled my opening then moved back to my clitoris, frantically flicking like he had some sort of fucking nervous twitch. Sighing and giving up, I pulled him up by his hair and pushed him back onto the bed. "I want to tie you up and slide my mouth down the length of your big cock."

He moaned loudly and moved up the bed until he rested on the headboard. "Go for it, sweetheart." He smirked as he rested his arms across the wooden spindles behind his head.

What a twat!

Yanking the belts from the two complimentary robes hanging on the back of the door, I grinned as I straddled his body and tied each of his wrists to the ornate bedposts, tightening the knots with expertise. I hunted in his suitcase which lay open on the floor, and grabbed a couple of his leather belts and secured his ankles to the bottom. His spread-eagled body made me shiver with anticipation.

He gasped when slowly I unzipped his trousers and pulled them and his briefs down over his legs, his dick springing free and slapping against his stomach excitedly. I was quietly impressed with his size; it was almost as big as his head. "Hurry up and suck my cock," he groaned, pulling agitatedly at his ties.

Tutting with a shake of my head, I slid his tie from his neck and stuffed it into his mouth, binding it harshly behind his head. He grumbled when the material cut into the edge of his lips, my unyielding tether painful. I chuckled and climbed off him.

He frowned, his rock hard cock still bouncing with his attempts to pull free when I pressed my dress back down and slid the long stiletto blade from my boot. His eyes widened when, very slowly, I ran the edge across my tongue, my heart beat shivering in delight when the taste of my own blood made my mouth water.

Sighing loudly, I shook my head in disappointment. "Your wife is very upset, Guy." He stilled instantly, staring at me like I'd told him I had four cocks dangling between my legs. Disgust, shock and alarm danced across his features. It was a shame; he really was good-looking. Such a loss. "It seems you've been a naughty boy. Very naughty. Lovely Kimberley has had enough of your infidelities."

His head shook rapidly, his eyes wet and pleading as they flicked from the knife casually twisting in my fingers then back up to my face.

"It seems you're worth quite a bit to her dead."

I couldn't help but roll my eyes at his pathetic whimper.

He wasn't as manly as he made out after all.

He tried to scramble away from me when I walked back over to him. Lifting his dick slightly with my little finger, I bent and kissed the tip. "Goodbye." Then I cut it off with one simple, clean swipe.

His tie drowned out his piercing screams, his tears pouring into his ears. Pulling a small box out of my bag, I took off the lid then placed his severed cock inside and popped the lid back on. Holding it up for him to see, not that he could really see through his dying tears, I grinned. "Little souvenir for her."

The blood forcefully pumping from his groin made me grimace. I didn't envy the cleaners. Oh well, not my problem.

"Well, take care." I saluted him then walked away.

Rogue pulled up at the front of the hotel when I walked out of the glass doors and slid into the passenger seat, "All done, gorgeous?"

"Yep, let's go party." I grinned as I pulled off the blonde wig and shook my black hair back onto my shoulders. "I've never been so bored in my whole life."

"That bad?" He glanced through his mirrors and pulled out of the carpark.

"God, the man was a knob." I chuckled. "Well, actually he's minus a knob now."

Rogue barked out a laugh and shook his head in amusement. "You never did?"

Patting my bag, I leaned my head back into the headrest and closed my eyes in comfortable appreciation. "A little gift for his wife… *widow*."

"Remind me to never piss you off." He smirked as he joined the motorway and took us south, home.

"You could never piss me off. You look after me too much for me to hurt you."

He smiled softly when I tilted my head and gazed at him adoringly. Rogue was like my big brother; he and Panther had taken me under their wing in the last two years. I knew Rogue wanted more from me but I could never give him something I didn't feel. That would hurt him more than me being insincere and slipping between the sheets with him. His smile dropped suddenly and he frowned to himself, glancing at me nervously. "What is it?"

He blew out a breath. "Panther rang me while you were inside."

"Yeah, and?" I didn't like his apprehension. Rogue was never edgy, and sensing his anxiety made me sit back up, my skin prickling.

His tongue swept around the inside of his cheek and he looked at me in the dim car. "Isaac's back."

My body stiffened involuntarily. My throat constricted and I swallowed the saliva that suddenly coated my mouth. "Okay."

"Is it?" he asked. "Okay, I mean."

Shrugging, I turned my face to the window and stared at the darkness outside. "Why shouldn't it be?"

"Well, you two got pretty close before…"

"Before he left," I finished. Then sighing, I looked at him. "It's fine, Rogue, really. It makes no difference to me. I'm not the girl I was before he left. I'm not naïve and I'm no longer fourteen. We shared a few kisses. That was it."

He nodded slowly. "I saw the way you used to look at him, Shadow. That wasn't just some odd snog to you."

"No, it wasn't, but that was two years ago. I killed my father… and my mother, and he walked away without even saying goodbye. Nothing could have hurt me more, and I have hardened since then. I told you, my heart isn't there for sentiment, it's just a tool to pump blood around my body. Nothing more, nothing less."

He smirked with a small chuckle. "You do know they call you the cold bitch back home?"

I shrugged. "They're right, and I don't give a fuck what they call me."

He glanced at me and sighed. "But I know different."

"No, you don't because I am exactly that. A cold bitch. There is nothing more inside me. It's okay, I know what I am, Rogue. You don't need to defend me."

He sighed loudly and shook his head. "Yeah whatever, Shadow. But I know deep down there's a heart in there that still bleeds with every breath you take."

"We bleed to breathe," I whispered sadly into the darkness, reciting half of one of the many Phantom aphorisms.

"And we bleed together," Rogue finished.

"Forever." I smiled as I slipped my hand into his when it came to rest on my thigh.

"Forever," he repeated almost painfully. "Always together."

Chapter Fifteen

'When the eyes don't see, the soul broods.'

BULLET HAILED ME when I walked into the communal area in West. "My bitch!" She winked at me as one of the new soldiers ran his tongue up the length of her neck. I couldn't help but roll my eyes. Hunter was smitten with my best friend.

I shouted something crude about her face and men's testicles, waving back as I snatched up a bottle of lager someone had craftily brought in, and downed half of it gratefully. Panther meandered over to me, his face pale and sad. My heart ached and I smiled softly. "How you doing, big guy?"

Shrugging, he looked away. I knew he was hiding his emotions – like we'd all been trained to do. Angered by his struggle, I gripped his arm. "You ever... *ever* need to let it out, you find me! I'm here, and it's between the two of us."

He swallowed heavily and blinked back his tears. He looked fraught with keeping his despair in and the horror of letting it all go. I nodded, encouraging him.

"Come find me. I'm just having a quick drink then I have

to report back to Frederik, but after that I'll be in my room."

He didn't answer me. I don't think he could form words, but he gave me a faint nod.

Woods, our brother, had been made an example of just ten days ago. He'd been given an assignment to slaughter a ten-year-old girl, and - like we all would have done - he covered up his aid to get her out of the country instead. Frederik had found out and made Woods' death as horrific and torturous as possible. All of West still had nightmares but Panther had lost his best friend and he wasn't coping well. However, we had been taught that emotions were a reckless weakness and we should never show our vulnerabilities. Panther was as tough as they came yet I could see him crumbling under the heartache. If he didn't let go, it would destroy what little of him was left.

Mouse grinned at me when I hugged her. "Happy birthday, sister." She knocked her bottle against mine and held it up, thanking me for my gift. We weren't allowed much but I'd been saving scraps of material from old clothes and bedding, and I'd made her a small patchwork throw for 'her' chair that was situated at the back of West's communal area. "One day, me and you will celebrate your birthday in the sunshine on some hot tropical beach in the middle of nowhere," I told her with a longing sigh. "We'll eat grilled shellfish by crystal clear blue water, drink cocktails with little umbrellas in, and get the hottest men to lather us in oil."

Rogue growled from behind me, his body pressing against my back as the music changed to a more upbeat track. "You know I'd willingly lather your little body in every sensuous oil known to man."

I swallowed as arousal flooded my belly, and I turned to smirk at him over my shoulder. "Oh, it will be a women only jaunt, Rogue. Just so we can go naked…"

"For fuck's sake," he grumbled as his fingers dug into my hips and he ground against me, his erection pressing against the small of my back. "Do you do it on purpose?"

Laughing, I finished off my lager and handed the empty bottle to him. "Always," I whispered, then sighing, I grabbed the little box from my bag and grimaced. "Wish me luck with the Lord and Master."

"You don't need luck," Tank said as he sauntered up to us. "You're the best sentinel in the family. Frederik won't get rid of you."

My head filled with visions of Woods and I swallowed back my own personal heartache. "You know that's not true, Tank. If I piss him off then I'm as gone as anyone else here. He pushes me more than any fucker here. The man hates every breath I take."

Bullet nodded. "Still doesn't mean he'll end you. Frederik is sly. He knows you bring in the money. He isn't stupid. Even though he's crueller with you than anyone, I honestly believe he'll never actually terminate you."

"Only time will tell, I suppose." My back itched, the reminder that I'd once more been under the fury of my master's flogger, my skin still raw at the memory of my loose mouth. I really had to start filtering what came out. I still struggled to contain my anger and I'd been flogged every night since I'd tackled Frederik over Woods' death. I'd even offered up myself to save my friend but, of course, Frederik wanted to watch me suffer. In a way, my friends were right. Frederik would never get rid of me; firstly, because I was his best assassin, but more importantly, I was his own personal punch bag. My pain was his pleasure. I refused to give in to his cruelty. I would endure his wrath over and over just for the knowledge that Mae still lived, and in the end, that's all that mattered.

"See you in the morning," I called out to the continuing party as I made my way to the north of the mansion.

The corridors were quiet, and I frowned at their emptiness. Usually, as the nights were our own, the large house was thriving with people milling about, but the quiet was disconcerting. However, when I entered the north quarters, the reason for the sparse population made itself clear.

Music played loudly, many people dancing in the centre of the communal area. Several tables were set to the side, each one brimming with food and drink. My stomach growled at the sight of all the luxurious nibbles, my mouth watering with hunger. One of West's punishments for our collaboration with Woods defection was no food for fourteen days, just minimum quantities of bread and water afforded to us. Luckily many of us could go for long periods without food, our bodies adjusted to how Frederik maintained them. But it didn't mean we weren't hungry. I'd been even luckier as my 'date' had fed me before I'd ended his life.

"Hey Shadow," Devlin greeted with a smile. "Everything go okay?"

"Perfect," I replied with a smile as he winked at me proudly.

Frederik stood at the top of the room. Even after nearly three years of being under his rule, my body still shivered with hatred and nerves in his presence. Frederik wasn't just our leader, he was our God. He was the one who decided if we deserved to repent for our sins, he was the one who decided if we lived or died. He was our creator.

He turned when he sensed my approach. His eyes, as always, narrowed on me.

"My assignment is complete, Master."

He took the box from me when I handed it to him. Without looking away from my eyes, he opened the box. "Did you come across any complications?"

"No Master. It went to plan."

A strange sensation slithered through me and I couldn't help but shiver. Warmth spread over my skin, my instincts alerting me to a watchful pair of eyes. Bewildered for a moment, I stood still and waited to be dismissed. Frederik eventually dropped his gaze to the box, then frowned. "What is this?"

The tone of his astonishment made my bones creak and I swallowed nervously. Maybe it hadn't been a good idea after all. "It's a gift for the investor, Master. I thought…"

My body flew sideways, my arm thudding against a concrete pillar when his fist connected with my cheekbone. "DID I GIVE PERMISSION FOR A FUCKING KEEPSAKE?" he roared as I gulped back the pain in my shoulder and quickly shuffled to my feet.

"No, Master. I apologise. It was presumptuous and forward of me."

Every single pair of eyes in the room were locked on me, some pitying but most eager for a show.

Frederik stepped towards me, pushing me backwards until my back slapped against the wall and another pain tore through my shoulder. I knew it was dislocated.

"You continue to defy me, Shadow. After everything, you still think you're above even me."

"No Master." I shook my head firmly. "I thought…"

I swallowed back the blood that filled my mouth when he hit me again. Pain exploded across my face and my teeth rattled with the rage fuelling my body. "Thoughts are gateways to rebelliousness, Shadow. How many times!"

"I'm sorry," I managed to spit out through the tightness of my jaw when he grabbed my neck and hauled me up.

Sighing in frustration, he shook his head in disappointment. "You know I will have to punish you for your insubordination."

"Yes, Master. I welcome my penance."

"You will meet Joel in the yard tomorrow at 4am."

Dipping my face graciously, I bit into my bottom lip. I hated Joel as much as I hated Frederik. Memories captured me in their cruelty and I shivered when horrified goosebumps rippled across my skin.

"Leave," he commanded.

"Master."

As I turned and I made my way out of the silent room, my pulse raced with what I knew the next day would bring. Bile threatened to make an appearance as my mind presented the many visions of what Joel would have planned for me. Damn it. It was just a dick for Christ's sake. A dead dick. I had completed the assignment, in record time I might add. I'd been given three days to complete it and it had taken me four hours.

Anger coursed through me as I stormed through the cold, empty corridors. One day I would flee, but not before I hacked off his fucking head and stuck it on a post in the yard for the crows to peck at. His reign would one day weaken him and that was the day I was holding on for; the time when I would bring the bastard down for his cruel dictatorship.

Panther frowned at me when I burst into my room. "Hey." He shot up off my bed and gawped at me. "What happened?"

"Fucking Frederik!" I growled when Panther grabbed my hairbrush and slid the wooden handle between my teeth. Manoeuvring my arm slowly, he pressed his thumb into my right shoulder and swiftly snapped my right back into place. Agony raged through me and my teeth sank unforgivingly into the piece of wood, decorating the handle with a pattern of my teeth. His large hands gently framed my face as he tenderly kissed my forehead.

"Okay?"

I trembled but nodded. "Yeah. Thanks."

Nodding, he passed me a plastic cup full of amber liquid and I necked it down in one go as he threaded a strap around my neck and gently looped it under my elbow to support my weak arm. Settling back on my bed, he supported his head with his arms and stared up to the ceiling. He was silent for a while but I could hear the depth of his despair.

He gripped my hand when I placed it onto his belly. Squeezing it, he sighed. "I can't do this anymore, Shadow."

I nodded. There wasn't anything to say because we all felt it. We all ached for the end. Life wasn't just cruel to us, it tormented us all, it mocked us with its refusal to end, and we all prayed for the end with an overwhelming yearning.

"He's at peace now, Panther. And in the end, it's all we can hope for."

The sound of his heartache tearing away from his soul made my throat close in and I struggled to breathe against the crushing thickness of it. He moved until his head rested in my lap and his hands clawed at me. I held him as tightly as I could, trying my best to hold him together as he broke.

"I miss him so fucking much that I'm struggling to breathe without him."

"I know," I whispered as my own devastation accompanied my friend's and my sobs became as fierce and consuming as his.

We held each other for a long time, both us us giving what we could as we took the comfort offered.

And when the clock in my room rolled up to 4am, I gently slid a sleeping Panther off my knee and went to repent for my sins.

Chapter Sixteen

'Regret is a wasted emotion. So is hope.'

Isaac

I WASN'T SURE HOW I felt about being back. After spending over two years with my uncle in Russia I had come to realise that my father's rule was beyond merciless. His tyranny was both oppressive and troubling. Artur, my uncle, my own father's brother, shared my concern. He wasn't as hateful as my father and the stories he had shared with me during our many drunken nights had made my conscience prickle with a burden I didn't want to carry.

My family originated just west of the cold Russian Ural Mountains, the harsh weather adding to the strict regime they ruled with. The Russian Mafia weren't to be taken lightly, and many years ago my father had thought he was above the family regulations. He had bedded his own brother's wife. Artur was, and still is, very family orientated. He believes that blood is the backbone of relations, and your blood comes before that of an outsider; yet this was his wife. Anyone else would have been slaughtered, but, instead, Artur had banished my father to England, to establish an association under the Phantom rule deep within the underworld of London. And unfortunately, he'd taken me with him.

Being with my uncle had shown me just how such an alliance should be governed. With strict fairness. Artur was known to all for his punishing regime but he also understood loyalty, something my father did not. Frederik saw all as a direct threat to him and the only way he thought he could keep control was to make everyone so fearful of him that loyalty wasn't even in the equation. It was a matter of live or die to every single Phantom.

Artur had sent me back after a few more incidents of my father's had come onto his radar. Although Frederik was my father, my ruler, Artur was in all respects the Phantoms Tsar, including mine, and I had returned to report back to him, or in easier terms, to spy.

It didn't sit well with me, but I recognised that Frederik's cruel ways couldn't go on, father or not. And if I hadn't figured that out for myself, watching him belt Shadow like he did last night had slammed it home. There hadn't been one single day when I hadn't thought about her. Her beautiful face, her striking blue eyes, her pretty smile, even her strength. However, on returning, I was shocked how different she was. No longer was she the quiet, timid girl. She was an assassin, and a damn good one if the stories about her were true.

Not much had essentially changed in my missing years, except her. Her underdeveloped teenage body had now filled out into stunning curves that made my dick hard and my mouth water. Although she was just under seventeen, she had the way of a knowing woman.

I'd dreamed of her often, her promise to me playing out in torturous detail until I'd come in my sleep like a pubescent teenager, my cum spread across the sheets upon waking every morning. And watching her walk into the party last night, I knew it was time to call her up on that promise.

Devlin smiled at me as I entered the West kitchen. "And the wanderer returns." Slapping me on the back, he pulled me into a hug. "I've kept things as smooth as possible for your return."

Giving him a grateful nod, my eyes slid around the kitchen. Frowning at the low count of Wests, I looked at Devlin. "Who's missing?"

His eyes glazed for a moment but he swallowed when I narrowed my eyes on him. Glancing at Panther, he sighed. "We lost Woods ten days ago."

"What happened?"

"He was given a contract on a ten-year-old. Couldn't do it."

Anger bubbled deep in my gut. Kids were out of the equation according to Artur, who had gone into a furious rage when I'd told him that Frederik didn't have those limits.

"There's still one missing." I had been searching for Shadow, and the knowing glint in Devlin's eye told me he knew it.

"Shadow is paying penance for..."

"For?"

"She was given an assignment to terminate a married man after he'd been cheating on his wife. Shadow cut his dick off and brought it back in a box."

My eyes widened and I stared at him, my lips twitching in humour. "Are you fucking kidding me?"

The others chuckled to themselves, all with their faces down to hide their amusement from me, but on catching my own laugh they looked up. Bullet smiled at me. "Good to have you back, Commander."

Nodding, I returned her smile. "I've missed you all too." Then turning to Devlin, I asked under my breath so the others couldn't hear, "How's Shadow doing?"

He looked at the floor then nodded. "She's become our top assassin."

"I didn't ask that."

"Yeah," he whispered as he grabbed my arm and pulled me to one side. "She seems to have become Frederik's personal prey. He hates her, Isaac. I've never seen him like this with anyone. Everything she does is never good enough, even though she is the cold, hard bitch that he wanted her to become. It's not enough for him. Nothing is ever enough where Shadow is concerned."

My heart threatened to stampede out of my chest and I clenched my jaw in attempt to slow it down. I knew she took the punishment for my affections towards her. Frederik had seen it and he'd brought his wrath on Shadow because of my inappropriate behaviour. To my father, he was more important than anyone, so watching me with Shadow, I knew he had become concerned that she would one day take over my affection for him. He had killed my own mother because I looked up to her more than I did him.

"Yet he hasn't executed her?"

Devlin scoffed and shook his head sadly. "That would be too easy on Shadow. She craves for death, Isaac, more than any other Phantom I've been charged with. She has a hunger for the end, yet she won't do it herself because Frederik told her he would take her sister if she ever walked away, even in death. Plus she's the hardest executioner he's ever seen. She can do a four day job in an hour. She's too valuable and too handy to knock about. He won't ever set her free, Isaac."

Something in my soul cried out in pain with Devlin's truths. The fact that Shadow wanted to die hurt me more than it should. I couldn't understand what the hell it was about that girl that got to me, but I was also accepting of the fact that she lived in me, in my soul, and even though I had done everything I could to drive her out, she was tethered to me so tightly it would be too painful to ever let her go. Truth be told, I didn't want to. I wanted her with an overwhelming need. I wanted to sink so far inside her that I gave her soul no chance to run from me. I wanted to capture her heart and only allow it to beat beside mine, and I needed her to look at me like there was no one else on the planet capable of making her feel good, capable of loving her. And I did. I loved her. But I could never tell her. Never. She could never see my weakness. That was something, even in love, I would not sanction. My vulnerability would sign her death warrant.

"Where is she?" I asked as I closed my eyes and attempted to push aside the incessant thud in my head.

"In the yard," Devlin said. "Joel is passing her sentence."

Nodding, I turned and walked away before he heard the growl rumble in my chest.

The rain beat heavy on the windows as I made my way to the courtyard, the gloom of the dark sky matching my mood. Many soldiers and sentinels dipped their heads respectfully as they passed me, the veterans whispering to the new recruits I hadn't met yet when they didn't respect my presence. It was all bullshit and I hated every damn second of it.

Thunder cracked in the sky as I stepped out into the large

square, but it couldn't be heard above the rage of my anger when Shadow came into view.

A pain tore through my chest as fury sucked me under. "What the fuck is this?"

All seven soldiers standing around the yard under umbrellas turned to me as soon as they heard my thunderous roar. Their eyes widened before they lowered them to the ground. "You!" I barked at one of them. "Get her down!"

His large round eyes flicked from me to Shadow and then back to me.

"Now!"

"Yes, Commander."

He ran across the grass to where she hung naked from the cross, however she wasn't just tied to it, she was fucking nailed to it. She was unconscious, the torrent of rain beating down upon her bleeding body. The rage inside me was bursting to get out, my teeth grinding together so hard I was worried they would crack under the force.

Wincing when the soldier took a damn claw hammer to her hands and yanked out the nails, I attempted to act calm and walked over to where Shadow lay in a heap under the cross. I removed my shirt and covered her body with it then scooped her up, pulling her into my chest, and swiftly walked back to my quarters, my senses going haywire with the feel of her next to me once again.

She murmured but didn't wake. However, when she snuggled deeper into me, I buried my face in her wet hair and placed a tender kiss to her forehead. Hating that once again I was at her mercy, I couldn't help but inhale her sweet scent. Even with the varnish of rain on her pale skin she still smelled the same as she had two years ago and my soul consumed everything my senses granted.

Yet when a word filtered into my head, I squeezed my eyes closed and shook my head in annoyance.

Mine.

Chapter Seventeen

'Retribution is a balm to the mind.'

Connie

PAIN AND THE delicious aroma of coffee woke me, my senses chaotic at the clash of agony and the promising nectar. My eyes felt heavy but I dragged them open when a sound brought me further into the realms of awareness.

For the longest moment I couldn't move – or breathe. Isaac had his back to me as he stood on the veranda with the double doors open wide, his head tipping back occasionally as he sipped from a steaming mug. Apart from some gym shorts, he was naked, the defined muscles and scars on his back moving every time he lifted and lowered his cup. His thick thighs seemed to ripple as the cold winter air tormented his skin, goosebumps erupting in a bid to fight off the cold. His jet black hair was messy, the top long and jutting out in clumps of wild rebelliousness.

My belly ached, my soul both weeping and singing with

the sight of him. I hated that he did this to me, despised myself for allowing him this much emotion after what he had done. Yet I couldn't deny what my heart craved.

I slowly lifted my hands. They were both bandaged, pain crippling me, but I pushed it back and slid out from under the sheet that covered me.

Sensing my movement, Isaac turned. Our eyes clashed and we both froze under the other's gaze. My mouth dried and my heart danced as once again his beautiful green eyes held me in their spell. Isaac rarely allowed his emotions to be seen, but for the briefest moment, regret and affection stared back at me.

Steam billowed from me in furious pants, the heat of my breath clashing with the icy air in the room. "Hello, Isaac."

He blinked, and everything he had just revealed to me disappeared in an instant. He crossed the room, his long strides both graceful and paced precisely until he came to stand before me.

I flinched when he lifted his hand and gently placed his palm on my cheek. I tried to resist him, I tried so hard, but the feel of his skin on mine was too much to deny and I closed my eyes and leaned into his gentle touch. My body roared to life under his devout attention, my soul energetic as it surged electricity through my tired body.

"What the fuck has he done to you?" he whispered, the pain in his voice too heavy to shoulder. I couldn't soothe his ache, nor did I want to.

"He took what you left behind."

Surprise covered his soft features as my words hit him, his gulp loud to my ears. "I never left you behind, Shadow. Not for one single second."

Anger distorted his gentleness when I pulled away from

his touch but my own resentment was too furious to push aside. I couldn't allow him in. I never allowed anyone in. Affection was a route to heartache and I knew that if my heart were to endure any more sorrow then my sanity would be lost forever.

I couldn't give him any words of comfort so instead I nodded and turned away, needing to distance myself from him before I caved to his touch again. It hurt so much that I longed to feel his caress but I was too hardened now to give him what he needed. I simultaneously detested what he had taken from me and craved what he could give me.

"Don't walk away from me, Shadow."

I shook my head without turning back to him. "I need to pay for my sins, Commander. Master will be furious that I haven't completed my punishment."

"What the fuck?" He growled as he snatched my wrist and twirled me back around to face him. "Since when have you called me Commander? And looking at you, you've paid for your sins with your damn fucking soul."

"That may be so, but it doesn't alter the fact that Master will make me pay again. I appreciate your intervention but unfortunately you have made my sentence invalid, and as such I will have to pay for that."

"Appreciate my intervention?" he barked incredulously. My formality confused him, I could tell, but what we'd shared two years ago was in the past, long gone, and I needed to keep it that way. "You don't need to worry about the consequences of *my* actions. Why are you being like this? Why aren't you being honest with me and yourself? I know you felt it too, Shadow. Don't refuse it."

"I'm sorry," I whispered, unable to control my emotions when he looked at me with so much despair that my heart clenched.

"I'm not your enemy, Shadow."

A bitter laugh spilled from me and tears filled my eyes. Blinking them back quickly, I stared at him. "You were always the enemy, Isaac. You should have killed me when you were sent to because this…" I flung my arm out, gesturing to the situation, not the room. "This is a torture worse than death. It's purgatory. *It's hell.* I'm a corpse being forced to keep fucking living and I can't…" A sob tore from me and I tried to swallow it back but it was too powerful and I knew if I kept it in it would kill me. "I can't breathe. *I don't want to fucking breathe!*"

Without warning, Isaac grabbed hold of me and pulled me to his chest when I broke before him. I'd expected his anger at my weakness but instead he whispered shushes in my ear as he carried me over to the bed and laid me down, his arms holding me tight as I let go. Why Isaac had the capability to make me so vulnerable, I had no idea, but shamefully, I clung to him in a bid to ease the misery that ravaged me.

"Let it go, my love. Let it go."

And I did. I used him as the torrent burst from me in waves of grief. I grieved for Woods, I grieved for Mae, I grieved for myself, but most of all I grieved for Isaac because he was as cheated by life as I was. I'd had the privilege of a good and happy childhood, whereas Isaac didn't have any happy memories to rely on. In a way, my losses were felt tenfold because I had something to compare to, but I was grateful for the things my mind held onto to give me solace in the lonely nights.

His hands framed my face just before his mouth met mine. My tears soaked our kiss, the saltiness of them bursting on our tongues when they met and twisted together. He moaned into my mouth when I ran my fingers through his thick soft hair, the pain in my palms unfelt when my fingers slid against the silky strands. His lips were soft and yielding and his kiss was firm and passionate, our need intensifying when he dropped his hand from my face and ran it delicately down my neck, my skin burning in the trail of his tenderness. His fingers gently brushed over my tingling skin, his touch gliding down until he cupped my breast over the material of the t-shirt he'd dressed me in.

Arousal flooded every part of me and I moaned with need as I pressed into his caress. His mouth left mine as he kissed down my neck, his tongue licking at my grief when he lapped at my tears and soaked up my sorrow.

A growl rumbled in his chest when I released his hair and dragged my nails down his bare back, relishing in the feel of his skin under my touch. His mouth found my nipple and he traced it with his teeth through the cotton shirt. My body roared with lust, his idolisation driving me wild with desire.

"Please," I begged when his hand slid between my thighs and I let my legs drop open, pleading with him to make me feel good.

Without saying anything, he kneeled up, his eyes blazing furiously as he pushed up my shirt and bared my nakedness to his gaze. His hungry eyes fed on me, his approval making my thighs wet as my belly trembled with need.

"Your body is fucking beautiful." His voice was choked but high as he ran his hands over my skin, his sorrow evident every time he passed over a particular scar. "Is it mine, my love?"

His words both broke me and thrilled me, but I nodded. "Yes. Take it."

Hungrily, his tongue ran the length of his lips before he

reached to the nightstand and grabbed a condom from the drawer. "You have no idea how long I've waited for this, Shadow."

My mouth watered and a needy groan left me when he ripped off his shorts. His cock was long and hard, the velvety shaft thick, and the end glistened with pre-cum. I realised he'd been circumcised and I wondered if it was a Russian custom, but when he slowly rolled on the condom, any thoughts left me as I waited eagerly for him to slide inside me.

Settling above me, he kissed along my jaw and positioned himself at my entrance. "I'll try not to hurt you, but I'm afraid when I break your hymen it's going to be painful."

He stilled when he felt me freeze beneath him, the tip of his cock still pressing against me. Rearing back, he narrowed his eyes on me. I couldn't look away from him, shame and horror making me numb and motionless.

He saw it and the pain that tore through me when he curled his lip and looked at me with disgust almost crippled me. "Shadow?" he asked tightly as he moved back and knelt between my legs.

Turning my head, I looked away from him but he snatched my chin in his fingers and forced my eyes to his. "Please tell me you didn't break your promise."

When I couldn't answer him, he closed his eyes in anger and stepped away from me. He yanked his shorts back on and sat on the edge of the bed, disappointment and fury coming from him in thick waves. "I don't…"

"I'm sorry," I whispered. Why I was apologising I had no idea, but as I reached out and touched him he flung himself away from me, turning my remorse into anger.

"Who?" he asked, his back to me as he stared at the wall.

"Does that matter?"

I gasped when he spun around and encircled my throat with a fierce grip. "You were mine, Shadow. You were promised to me. So yes, it matters. It fucking matters a lot." His hold was punishing and I couldn't move. He wouldn't allow me to shift from his grip and his glare.

Furious at my own shame, I stared at him. What gave him the right to treat me like an object? He was no better than the others and suddenly my fury was beyond restraint. "How dare you!"

He scoffed, his outrage cruel as his eyes roamed my body with disgust blazing brightly. "How dare I?" he countered, "How dare *I*? You don't even care, do you? So come on, Shadow!" he snarled as he spat the words in my face when he pressed against me, his nose squashing against mine. "Who had your virginity?"

"It doesn't…"

"WHO?" he roared.

And I snapped.

"I have no idea!" I cried out. "I passed out when their torture became too much… right before they raped me!"

He froze. My heart thudded in the stillness of my body. I don't think I was breathing as my outburst threatened to annihilate us both.

"T-They?"

The vomit in my throat restricted my voice and I scrambled back when Isaac let out a horrific howl.

"WHO?" he shouted. "Who was there?"

I slapped my hand over my mouth to force back the vomit and the sob that begged for freedom. I daren't answer him. He was beyond furious, his rage making the marrow in my bones freeze with terror. I'd heard stories of Isaac's madness but until then I'd never witnessed it. And now I had, I wanted to hide from it. I wanted to run from it and never look back.

He closed his eyes for a long time and I watched as he battled to get his emotions back in check. When he opened them, the grief held there was as agonising as my own. His grip on me softened and he cupped my face so tenderly the sob that I had strived to keep in broke free in a wretched wail.

"I'm sorry," I cried. "I'm so sorry. I couldn't… they… I tried to stop them. I tried to keep my promise but…"

"Shh," he breathed as he pulled me into his body. "Shh, you have nothing to be sorry for. I'm sorry." He sighed and held me tighter. "When?" he asked when I clung to him and took his comfort.

"The day you left. I was bound to the cross for a week as punishment for my mother's death."

He tensed. "Was it… my father?"

I looked up at him and shook my head quickly. "No. No, Master has never touched me like that."

He blinked at me, confused by my revelation. "Then who was in charge of your punishment?"

My mouth dried and I argued with myself for a long time. I wanted to tell him, but equally I didn't. I despised myself for feeling shame at what they did but I didn't want to burden Isaac with it. Yet I knew he would never allow me to keep this secret from him. "Joel," I whispered.

He moved so fast that the backdraft from him caused me to gasp. He was out of the door before he'd even fastened his jeans. Terror consumed me and for the first time in a long time, I felt fear. Fear for what Isaac would do, for what repercussions would come from his need for vengeance against something he had always considered his - me.

And as I sat there in the silence of his room, I knew that

the end was now inevitable. For both of us. And I prayed for it.

Chapter Eighteen

'We cross the line, then we pay the fine.'

Isaac

EAST'S COMMUNAL AREA became silent when I walked in calmly. All eyes turned to me before Joel turned around. His smile was large, his delight at my return evident.

"Hey, man," he said as he walked over to me. "It's good to have you back."

He frowned when he slapped me on the top of the arm and I stiffened with disgust. Becca, now his second, watched me with curiosity. She could see it in me, the wrath that threatened to consume my soul.

"What's wrong with you?" Joel scoffed as though offended by my detachment towards him, but I could smell his fear; it stank and curdled the breakfast that lay heavily in my gut.

Everyone was rigid with apprehension as they watched me. Tipping my head slightly to the side, I narrowed my eyes on him. I couldn't figure out exactly when my best friend had become such an animal. I knew he loved this life but he'd stepped over a line that couldn't be restored. He'd not only broken my trust, he'd severed any loyalty I had towards him.

"I asked you to do one thing, Joel."

He froze, his mouth open as he looked at me vigilantly. "Yes."

He gulped when I stepped into him. I was struggling to hold it all back. I was always in control of my temper but this time it was massacring me from the inside. Visions froze my blood, images of my best friend taking something I had cherished. He couldn't be allowed to breathe for what he had done to Shadow.

"Let's remind ourselves what that was, shall we?"

Fury ghosted his face but he knew he was no match for me. Pursing his lips, he snorted. "You fuck off for two years then think you can swan back in and treat me like shit?"

Rage stimulated every organ in my body as I fought to pull back but when he shrugged casually and foolishly disregarded my anger, I allowed the ice to trickle into my bones.

"I don't know what your problem is, anyway. You asked me to watch over her, Isaac. You didn't say I couldn't have her."

Every single person in the room gasped when Joel's back hit the wall and my blade held his throat hostage. "You vicious little cunt. She was fourteen, you sick fuck! I hope you know I'm going to ram your dirty fucking dick right down your rancid throat."

He trembled under me, his terror exposed openly on his face. "Fuck, man, I..."

"I want every name. Each and every person who broke my girl."

"Your girl," he scoffed. "Your girl? Shit, man, what the

fuck is wrong with you?"

"*You're* fucking wrong with me." Narrowing my eyes, I pressed the edge of my blade deeper into his flesh, a trickle of blood easing my anger slightly when it oozed down the centre of his throat.

"Isaac?" Becca came to stand beside me but I ignored her.

"Names!" I roared.

"Fuck you!"

When a sinister smile crept over my face, the stench of Joel's piss filled the air. "Wrong answer," I whispered.

Just as I started to slide the knife over his jugular, every nerve in my body tingling in delight, my father bellowed into the cold silence of the room. "ISAAC!"

My hand shook with need, my teeth clenching as I battled to stop my knife from carrying on its needful slaughter.

"STOP!" Frederik boomed again. "You of all Phantoms know the punishment for killing one of our own."

I was vibrating with hunger for retribution, my body so sensitive with need it was agonising. "Death," I replied in a quiet hiss. "But please remind me why that conclusion doesn't seem so fucking problematic right now?"

Becca moved away quickly as Frederik marched up to me and gripped my wrist in his fingers. Quietly and chillingly, he chuckled, "And you're willing to give *your girl* over to me, are you?"

As much as I longed for death, I knew I couldn't leave Shadow in the fate of such an evil bastard. He would make her pay for this, for my loss of control.

Joel's wide eyes stared at me, begging me to listen to my father. I wanted to stab the tip of my knife through each of his eyeballs for even looking at me.

"Isaac," Becca begged softly, her soft touch on my back

finally breaking through to my sanity. "He's not worth it."

"Fuck!"

They all watched my back when I stormed out of the room, Joel's gasp of relief making me smile to myself.

He thought it was over. The fucking fool.

Chapter Nineteen

'The longer we wait, the sweeter the reward.'

THE TWO HOUR run had done nothing to reduce my anger, or my hard on. I'd been as hard as granite since the tip of my cock had pressed so fucking gloriously against Shadow's soft, hot flesh.

Oddly, for the first time ever, I felt regret. Regret for not digging Joel's tonsils out with my blade, and guilt about how I had treated Shadow when she'd told me the promise she had given me three years ago was now an impossibility. Much to my disgust, I'd made her feel like a leper. I'd seen it in the way she'd looked at me, and heard it in her apologetic whimpers.

Phantom life was cruel and unforgiving, but there were some acts that were considered sick and off limits. One was having sex with a child, and the second was rape. Joel had broken both those rules and he would pay. I would make sure of that, even if it cost me my life.

The West kitchen was full when I walked in and all heads turned to me. Devlin, sensing my mood, cocked his head.

"You okay?"

Without answering his question, my gaze roamed the soldiers and sentinels eating breakfast. I growled in annoyance at the meagre servings of bread delivered by the main kitchen for West's rationed portions.

Pulling my wallet out, I threw fifty quid at Devlin. "Go fetch pastries in."

He frowned at me. "What?"

My temper was already simmering under the surface and his hesitation made it start to boil over. "Don't question me, Dev, just do. Or can't you manage to sneak food past the sentries?"

His eyes widened at my mockery and he held up his hands in surrender. "You know I can, and that isn't what's worrying me. *You* are worrying me, not me getting fucking caught."

"Well let me ease that pressure for you – don't. It's about time things fucking changed around here."

All eyes watched me cautiously but Devlin's were full of apprehension. Grabbing my arm, he pulled me to one side and lowered his voice. "What the hell does that mean? Don't tell me you're planning on going up against your father. He won't tolerate your insubordination, Isaac."

"Well maybe it's about time he saw just what his cruel fucking rule twists people in to." Cutting him off before he could answer, I turned back to the others. "Where's Shadow?"

"Showers," Bullet divulged as Rogue scowled at me.

"Why?" he asked.

The other soldiers stiffened, and even Mouse's eyes widened on his sharp demand. I couldn't help but grin at his jealousy. Stepping up to him, I smirked in his face. "Because I'm going to fuck her until she can't remember her own name, and she screams mine. What that has to do with you, I have no idea. You're welcome to watch if that's your thing but I'm not sure Shadow would appreciate it."

The fury spitting from him was almost comical. He was head over heels in love with her and if he hadn't just riled me up then I could have felt sorry for him, but the prick needed to learn his place. I snatched his jaw in a rough grasp and snapped his head back until he had no choice but to look at me. "Shadow is off limits. Understand?"

His teeth clenched as he tried to rein in his rage and his chest heaved as his furious gulps for air made him tremble under my hand.

"Do – you - understand?"

"Yes, Commander," he hissed.

Dropping him as quickly as I'd seized him, I walked out before I lost control and smashed his face against the table, and forced the cheap veneer down his fucking throat. I was losing my shit all over the place and I knew if I didn't sort myself out quickly I'd be entertaining Frederik's famous long blade. My body vibrated with need, and by the time I'd stormed through the west wing's corridors to the shower block, I was humming with a primal craving for release.

The lust riding me suddenly became uncontrollable when I walked into the showers. Her back was to me, her face pointed upwards into the spray of the water. The pale expanse of her tight arse was pure heaven to my sore eyes, the curve of it absolute perfection. The groove of her spine called out to me, my tongue wetting my lips hungrily as I imagined sliding it slowly up the length of scar tissue until my mouth found the nape of her neck.

As I yanked off my clothes, she sensed me and turned. Her eyes didn't widen in surprise, nor did her face show any shock at my presence. Instead, her scorching eyes locked onto mine before I dropped my gaze and my eyes slid down the whole of her beauty.

Her tits heaved as she gulped in air, her deep pink nipples fat and hard as water spilled down her chest in rivulets then across the flat of her stomach, and finally down into the bare apex of her thighs.

She stood still as I closed the gap between us but when I reached her, my legs still moving, she backed up until her back hit the wall and she looked up at me.

"Do you know how happy my cock is with you right now?"

She blinked at me and bit her lip to stop her grin. "Not as fucking delighted as my pussy is with you."

She gasped when I pinched her throat in a fierce grip, her pupils dilating when an animalistic need stared back at me. Her pulse raced in the palm of my hand and her chest heaved so much that her rigid nipples brushed against the covering of hair on my chest.

As soon as I slammed my mouth over hers, her legs wrapped around my waist and her arms slid around my neck. She moaned into my mouth, begging me when I roughly cupped her firm tits and pressed her back into the tiles to support us both.

Her cunt was wet and her slick arousal lubricated the shaft of my cock as I thrust my hips and slid it along the groove of her swollen lips. My balls drew back so hard I thought they'd be lost forever when she rocked against me, using me to pleasure herself, her soft whimpers driving me crazy.

"Look at me, Shadow."

She snapped her eyes open and gazed up at me. For a moment I was lost in the pure blue depths reflecting so much emotion that I was scared to breathe in case it evaporated before I could get my fill of it. There was so much more than desire looking back at me, and a tortured growl rumbled deep inside me when a raw possessiveness slammed deep inside my soul. I knew right then that I would protect her with my life, that I would trade my very last breath to grant her another. She wasn't just a fuck, a conquest. She was a gift.

"Next time I'll be slow, but right now I can't give you that."

"So there will be a next time?"

Slowly nodding, I pressed against her and gradually sank deep inside her glorious hot cunt until my balls squashed against her and my pelvis rubbed over her swollen little nub of nerves. *Holy shit!* She drew in a long breath and her mouth fell open as I rested my face into the crook of her neck for support. "Oh yeah, there'll be a next time," I breathed through clenched teeth. "And a next time, and a next time."

Her pussy dragged me deeper. She was so tight and hot that I worried I wouldn't get her to orgasm before I exploded deep inside her.

My legs were trembling so I lowered us to the floor, the water cascading over us as Shadow took precedence and started to move on me. Her mouth found mine as she whimpered into me, her tongue swirling and twisting with my own as she fucked me harder and faster. Her tits rubbed up and down my chest, her nipples taking the pleasure as her frenzied need for release drove her harder on me.

Taking her plump nipple between my teeth and biting down, she cried out in pleasure as an orgasm ravaged her and her body shook over me. Her tight walls milked me dry, forcing the cum from my balls in a painful ecstasy so white hot that I couldn't hold back the roar of pleasure as I burst into her, my hips pumping and driving my cock deep inside her.

We panted hard, the water washing away the sweat that covered us both. She buried her face into my neck and softly kissed me. "I'm glad you're back," she whispered.

Lifting her face to mine with a finger under her chin, I kissed the tip of her nose. "Me too. Things are going to change, Shadow. I promise I won't let him hurt you anymore."

She tensed and lowered her eyes, however she nodded then settled back against me. I had a feeling she didn't believe me but I would show her. She needed someone to trust after all she had lost, and I swore that would be me.

"I'll protect you with my soul, my love." I just hoped it wasn't too late to save her own.

Chapter Twenty

*'We pay with more than just our souls.
We pay with every one of our impending breaths.'*

Connie

GRABBING A TOWEL, I rubbed my face with it, wiping away the sheen of sweat plastered to my red face. My morning routine had taken a serious nosedive. Isaac's animalistic sexual appetite through the night had left me with little energy for the four mile run I tortured my body with every morning without fail.

I couldn't help but smile as I dipped under the cold spray. My body hummed with satisfaction. Isaac was so giving in bed that the numerous orgasms he'd given me had left my body stimulated to a point of sensitivity, the pounding shower making the many bruises on my body throb deliciously.

I stilled when I saw Becca slide under the adjacent shower to me. I could feel her stare on me, her eyes raking down my body and leaving a burning trail in their path.

"Morning, Shadow."

I tensed at her pleasant tone. I'd been expecting her hatred but surprisingly, I didn't get it. "Hey, Becca. You okay?"

She smiled and nodded before lifting her face to the icy cascade. I couldn't help but allow my eyes to take in her perfect figure. She was supple and toned, her own skin free of scars and blemishes, the result making her enviously perfect. Her breasts were high and firm, her stomach flat and muscular.

When I lifted my eyes back to her face, I found her watching my observation with a knowing gaze. Then, as I had, her own eyes dropped and she slowly dragged them down my nakedness. Shamefully, the heat in her study made my nipples harden and my pussy slick outrageously. My belly warmed and my lips parted to accommodate my heated breaths.

What the fuck?

Once her gaze had found mine again, she narrowed her eyes on me, not in an angry stare but a curious one and stepped from under her own shower and into my own. Shocked, I froze, her closeness making me weirdly nervous. She was so close that I could feel her breath on my cheek. However, when she leaned into me and dragged the tip of her tongue over my collarbone, her eyes locked onto my face, I couldn't help but shiver under the tenderness of her touch.

"Have you ever been with another woman, Shadow?"

"No," I whispered immediately. I had meant it to warn her off but the choked way it came out made her smirk.

My belly ached with pressure when she ran her tongue down between my breasts and softly placed a kiss to the swell of flesh beside my nipple.

"You're simply quite beautiful," she breathed as her tongue flicked over my rigid nipple. "I can see why Isaac is smitten."

Then just as quickly, she stepped away, grabbed her towel and left the shower block, leaving me trembling.

Mortification controlled me, my whole body flushing at my reaction to her. I knew most of the female Phantoms often indulged in lesbian sex but I'd never before felt anything like I just had with Becca. Another concern was that I hated the bitch; she was mean and cruel to the new soldiers, making sure that they knew she was above them.

Putting it down to the hormones still running my body after the night's fuckfest with Isaac, I shook it off and made my way back to my room. It was still early and usually I was the only one up at that hour, but quite a few people milled about. A couple of people lowered their eyes when I walked passed them and I frowned to myself. Generally everyone was friendly with me but the more they either looked away or whispered as I walked passed, the more my skin prickled with anxiety. There was a strange buzz in the air and the closer I got to the corridor which housed all of West's bedrooms, the more difficult it became to breathe.

My footing stumbled when, turning the corner that led into the hallway, I saw everyone was standing outside Mouse's room. Bullet's grief-stricken wail ricocheted off the bare walls and slammed inside my chest.

"No."

Rogue grabbed me when I broke into a run and pushed through the congregation. "No, Shadow."

"Get off me!" I hissed as I yanked out of his hold and burst into Mouse's room.

My legs gave way and I fell to my knees on her floor as an agonising cry tore up my throat with a wave of vomit. My head shook as tears blurred her broken and tortured body.

She was face down on the bed, blood leaking from every orifice on her bruised and mauled body as her dead eyes stared at the wall where a message had been left for me in Mouse's blood.

> You squeal, your friends pay.

Panther tried to drag me away when I bundled Mouse up and sat rocking her, whispering with frantic apologies in her unhearing ears. "I'm so sorry, Mouse. Oh God, forgive me. I'm so sorry."

"It's not your fault, Shadow," Panther tried. But it was. It was. I'd told Isaac what Joel had done.

Cement slowly trickled into my veins. My tears stopped, my heart beat slowed and an icy sludge slid into the marrow of my bones. Tenderly, I laid Mouse back down, my palm respectfully closing her eyelids. I kissed her on the forehead, told her I loved her and then went in search of Joel.

Chapter Twenty-One

'Payback is a bitch.'

Isaac

"WHERE THE FUCK is she?" I barked at all of West as they stood with red-rimmed eyes watching me go crazy. "FIND HER!" They all scattered in different directions as I stabbed at the keys on my phone, dialling her number and growling in frustration when I was greeted with a long continuous tone yet again. "Come on, my love. Where are you?"

Devlin stared at me and shook his head. "It's a fucking mess." His eyes dropped to Mouse's body. I'd liked Mouse, she'd been a good soldier. She had been feisty, hence her lack of tongue when she'd mouthed off at my father once, but she could take orders and follow them through without a second thought. But at that moment, I was more concerned for Shadow. She'd disappeared hours ago after finding her friend, the words smeared on the wall obviously a message for her after she'd told me what Joel had done to her.

Joel was dead. It was that simple. I was going to snap his neck quickly and cleanly.

"We need to figure out how we're going to handle this." Devlin sighed sadly. He too had been fond of Mouse and it hurt when we lost one of our own.

Dragging my hands over my face, I replied with a nod. I was exhausted. I'd been inside Shadow all night, her perfect little body and sexy moans had made me take her over and over again. She'd been as tight and hot as I had known all along she'd be. Three years I had waited for her, and the wait had been more than worth it. However, I didn't like how she also affected my emotions. A fuck was a fuck, but with Shadow it was different. I couldn't pinpoint what it was about her, but I knew she had gotten under my skin. The way she looked at me, her eyes sparkling with something other than pleasure had made the beat of my heart speed up and the need to satisfy her grow until all I could concentrate on was making her come with an overwhelming ecstasy.

"Take her out and find a secluded site," I said to Devlin as we both continued to stare with sadness at Mouse. "Don't be seen."

He nodded as I left him. I needed to find Shadow. Where the fuck was she? I just prayed that she hadn't done something stupid. I knew she wanted to leave our torturous life, and it was only because of her sister that she was still there. My heart clenched when I knew this could push her over that line into the inhumane Phantoms we all became after time.

The corridors were bursting with people as the start of the day saw many Phantoms begin training or receiving their specific assignments. My father had called for my presence, most likely to receive my own orders, but he'd have to wait until I sorted this shitstorm out. He couldn't find out about

Mouse or we'd all pay for what Joel had done.

Quickly answering my phone when Rogue's name scrolled up, I stiffened when apprehension controlled the tone of his voice. "You better come to the courtyard."

Without answering him, I pocketed my phone and broke into a run. I would lose my shit if Joel had hurt her and bound her to the cross again. I was just waiting for the time to end him without the fall-back of it coming back to me.

However, when I entered the courtyard, I realised my worries had been completely the wrong way around.

"Holy shit!"

Rogue's worried stare found me and he winced. "I can't find her," he whispered.

The blood in my veins froze as my eyes beheld the scene before me. Joel was nailed to the cross. A cavity in his chest displayed the void inside, his heart now slapped at the base of his feet and his toes tinged with the colour of his own blood. His naked body missed an essential part but as my eyes lifted to his face, I found it. His dick was protruding from his open mouth, a silent scream evident on his dead face.

"Fuck!" Bullet's gasp broke me from my horrified stare and I turned to her.

"Did you find her?"

She shook her head, her wide eyes still fixed on Joel. "Shit." She chewed on her lips for a moment then looked at me. "I might know where she is."

"Tell me."

Nodding, her stare once more fixed on Joel. "Down by the stream there's a secluded spot between the two big trees. She often goes there when she needs to be alone."

Looking at Rogue, his sadness made my gut twist. "I'll find her," I told him as I slapped him on the shoulder.

He nodded. "I'll see to Joel."

Giving him a nod of thanks I tore from the courtyard and made my way down to where Bullet had told me.

As soon as I pushed through the heavily laden trees I saw her. She was sat cross-legged, staring into the fast flowing water. My heart surged when I noticed she was still covered head to foot in Joel's blood.

"Hey, love," I whispered as I walked up behind her hesitantly.

Her head turned, and what greeted me sliced something deep inside, the pain in her eyes making my breath catch in my throat. "I'm sorry," she choked out. "I'm so sorry."

"Hey," I said as I sat beside her and pulled her to me. She curled up and pressed against me, her heartbroken whimpers making my soul weep with her. "Shh."

"Will you try and save Mae?"

Tensing, I tipped her head back, making her look at me. "It won't come to that, Shadow. I won't let it."

She smiled sadly. "You know he will kill me for this Isaac. Please accept it and grant my request. I know he will go after Mae after my death." A sob broke from her and she squeezed her eyes closed. "I couldn't allow him to live for what he did to Mouse. He should have come to me. Making my friends pay is cowardly and unforgivable."

"I know," I said as I held her tighter.

She was right; Frederik would make her death painful for this. We never, ever took one of our own out. It was in the rules; the very first rule. Only my father was granted permission to terminate a Phantom. And Shadow would pay with her life.

But I wouldn't allow that. My father would believe it was me who killed Joel. As much as I wanted to free her from this life, I wanted so much more than death for her. I wanted her to live, and I prayed that one day, even without me, she would be able to look up to the sky and smile. And as I lifted Shadow back off my knee and placed her back on the grass, I pressed my mouth to her forehead. Knowing what I had to do came easy to me, and it made me recognise the feeling that beheld me over Shadow. I was in love with her. But she could never know.

"I'll be right back. Stay here," I breathed into her hair as I closed my eyes and inhaled her sweet scent to memory. It seeped into me, calming the erratic beat in my chest and soothing the pain of what I had to do. I needed it to make my next journey bearable. I needed her unique scent to carry me into hell.

Chapter Twenty-Two

'The very things we do for love will one day kill us.'

Connie

ISAAC DIDN'T RETURN as I sat there between the trees, watching the sun disappear behind the horizon. I wanted to go with it, follow its path down under the ground and welcome the darkness. My heart beat furiously in my chest, yet I didn't want to feel it anymore. I wanted it to still, to take one last beat and leave me to slither into hell.

I was so tired, my body trembling with exhaustion, my soul subdued and begging for freedom. My insanity had become the very thing that kept me alive, the torture it lived through driving my heart to keep pumping blood around my body.

Finally pushing my weary body up, I blew out a breath and went to accept my fate.

The Phantom home was quiet when I slipped back in. It was supper time but I didn't bother heading to the dining area in the southern section. I wouldn't be fed again, and strangely, the calmness that saturated me and granted the constant pain a reprieve didn't want to be fed. I wanted to leave this earth hungry because that was the only thing I could feel right then. My heart still beat, my soul still held my spirit up, and my mind still placed random thoughts in my head, but I didn't feel any of those things. Numbness and detachment shielded my despair from my upcoming death.

I thought of Mouse, Woods, and my mother on the slow walk. I smiled. For the first time in a long while, I smiled. I was eager to be with them, to be taken from this horrific life and finally feel the heat of hell on my skin. I knew without a doubt they wouldn't be there to welcome me, but my mind played with scenarios where, once a year, heaven and hell joined to party and welcome in the New Year together. I laughed at that thought, the faint chuckle the only sound in the empty corridors as I took the journey to my master.

I frowned when, on entering Master's quarters, an eerie silence welcomed me. Master's quarters filled the entire north section. It was split into two; the front section where he conducted his business, and the locked and secured part where no one ever ventured was to the rear behind a door. We all speculated about how regal it would be, and what actually went on behind that door, but in reality, none of us wanted to find out.

A group of people stood in a circle surrounding something, and when Isaac turned to me, his eyes wide and worried upon seeing me, my body shivered with anguish.

"What's going on?"

Isaac swiftly walked to me, his long legs pacing him quickly, and he took my hand then pulled me out of the room. "Isaac?"

He didn't speak to me as I strained to look over my shoulder at what was going on. I squinted when I managed to see a part of someone on the floor through a gap in the mass of legs, a shock of black hair and what looked like a pool of blood against the paleness of the ivory floor tiles.

"Isaac?" I panicked, pulling out of his grip as I raced across the room. My heart exploded when I saw Rogue's head sitting a foot from his body, a pond of his blood the only thing joining it to the neck of his body. "NO!"

Isaac caught me when the world went black and I fell to the ground, the dead eyes of my friend the last thing that I saw before the abyss welcomed me.

It all became too much. Upon opening my eyes, I didn't want to accept that my life went on after the death of Mouse and Rogue. I wanted to follow my friends. I wanted them to take my hand and escort me on the journey they had taken. I couldn't breathe through the agony of grief clutching at every organ inside me.

Isaac held me, his silent support giving me more than he could ever imagine. "I want to go with them," I whispered as I rocked with the pain of their deaths. "I – want –to –go – with –them! I can't do this anymore."

The sobs that tore from me hurt my ears and I curled even deeper within myself, hating the sound of my defencelessness. Three years of suffering burst from me in a current of snot and tears and pain and misery. I longed for Mae, for my mother, for life beyond the realms of this living hell.

"I can't…" I wept and vomited at the extent of it all. But Isaac just held me, his strong arms protecting me from myself, his many kisses in my hair soothing the cruel bite inside my skull as insanity corroded my mind.

My body ached with devastation and my bones splintered against the punishing crush of my broken soul. When would it ever end? When would God finally grant me peace and take me away from a life that ripped everything from me in unrelenting barrages of mercilessness? There was nothing left of me, nothing inside me that could carry me through the rest of my days. After everything that the last three years had tormented me with, Mouse and Rogue's death had finally taken the last part of my strength and annihilated it.

"Why Rogue?" I whispered as my body shook with despair. "Why Rogue?"

"He loved you," Isaac whispered after a long silence.

His words and the whispered way he said them made me lift my eyes to his. Isaac stared down at me, his eyes telling me what he couldn't voice. Bile hit the back of my throat and I narrowed my wet eyes on him as my head shook from side to side. "No," I hissed out as I scrambled away from him, the realisation of what Rogue had done hitting me with a force that winded me. "Tell me he did not… he didn't… please…."

When Isaac lowered his eyes and nodded, the world around me died right along with me. "He loved you, Shadow. Enough to die for you."

My vision blurred when I tore into Isaac as the pain inside me became unbearable, my lungs burning with the deluge of pain surging through me. "NO!" I screamed as my fists laid into him. "No!"

I couldn't breathe as everything broke from me in a swell of hatred and rage. "This is your fault! It's all your fault. You should have killed me!" I cried as my punches continued to break his skin. "You should have killed us both! I hate you! I hate you!"

My mother. Mouse. Rogue. My father. They all died at my hands. All of them were dead because of me. And I deserved to follow them.

"I have to tell Frederik."

Isaac chased after me as I ran from the confines of his bedroom, his arms wrapping around me as he stopped me in my mission. "Get off!" I shouted as I struggled in his hold. "I deserve to be with them all."

I gasped when Isaac's firm hand slapped my face, my head spinning to the side with the force of his slap. "Rogue died so you didn't!" he bellowed at me, his anger now as intense as my desolation. "I was willing to die for you! I tried, Connie! I tried but I was too late!"

My name from his mouth froze my body and I stared up at him.

"Don't throw his love back," he whispered as his hands framed my face tenderly. "Don't make his death a mockery. You go and tell Frederik it was you who killed Joel then everything Rogue did was a waste of his life. Honour him, Connie. Accept the gift he wanted you to have."

His mouth crushed against mine, his tongue seeking out my tears and taking them from me. His arms pulled me tight against him, his devotion to me smothering the pain that cursed me and granted it peace.

"Carry on living," he whispered as he grabbed the hem of my t-shirt and lifted it over my head. "Use what Rogue gave you. Be the Phantom I need you to be."

My fingers slid into his hair when his teeth trapped my nipple through the cotton of my bra and he tugged. Dropping to his knees before me, he unbuttoned my jeans and pushed them down my hips, exposing my wet flesh to his mouth. He ate me like a religious man starved of bread and water, his worship on my throbbing cunt breaking my insanity and bringing me to my knees, where he pushed me back, ripped off my jeans and continued his idolisation. Orgasm after orgasm took me to the gates of heaven and back as he feasted on every drop of arousal that flooded his mouth.

And when he slipped me over onto my stomach and pressed his thick cock against my arse, I nodded. "Take me there," I pleaded. "Please."

"Have you ever?"

Shaking my head, I looked over my shoulder at him. "I've never been loved there." His eyes widened on me. He knew what I meant. My anal virginity had been taken from me in a horrific way. "I need you to give me back the pleasure."

He gazed at me for a moment and I wasn't sure if he was angry or sad. Maybe both. But he lifted to his feet and rummaged through a drawer, coming back to me with a small bottle of what looked like oil. He kissed his way down my back, his tongue tracking each welt and I shivered when I felt a cold trickle between my buttocks.

"Relax, my love," he urged when he slipped a finger into my backside and I tensed. "I promise I'll make you feel so good."

I trusted him, the only person I could ever trust in this sad life, and I did as he asked, making my body relax into the thickness of the lush carpet that covered his once hard floor. My body tingled with pleasure when he pressed two fingers into my pussy and worked my arse until I moaned loudly and pushed myself harder onto him.

"Ready?" he asked gently as his nose nuzzled into the dip

of my ear. Nodding, unable to speak, I pressed my backside into his groin, encouraging him.

My fingers clawed at the carpet as he slid his cock into my arse, the pressure overwhelming as he nibbled at the soft skin on my neck. "Oh fuck," I panted as he pushed slowly all the way in until the fullness made me catch a breath.

"Jesus holy hell," he hissed out as he drew the tip of his nose across the nape of my neck. "You okay?"

I moaned, meaning to say yes but all that came out was a voice of my pleasure. So I nodded again. He drew out of me so slowly I had to clench my teeth against the sensation of it, but when he pressed back in, I lifted my bottom and the angle seemed to accommodate him a little more. Isaac was big, his cock fat and long, and I was apprehensive that he might tear me but his tender devotion to pleasuring me made me writhe in bliss beneath him. Sensing my need for more, he sped up slightly, his cock sliding in and out of my arse so perfectly paced that the feeling of him pushing and pulling built a climax so quickly I choked on my own scream when it suddenly burst inside me.

"Shit, Connie!" he cried out.

A sob tore from me at the sound of my name once again leaving him with his loss of control. Isaac was always so disciplined with his feelings, and I realised that when he was emotional he couldn't control what he said, hence my real name bursting from him as his own orgasm took him into the sphere of ecstasy. And I gave him that. I made him feel so good that he lost control. And that, with the wave of bliss rolling over me, brought me back over the edge until I was screaming his name with the heat of rapture that gripped every bone in my body.

I had fallen in love with the man who had taken so much

from me. I had loved him for such a long time that when he rolled over onto his back, groaned and broke wind, I just sighed and rolled my eyes. Love is a strange thing.

Chapter Twenty-Three

'Good surprises. Bad surprises. They all surprise us.'

Connie

February 2008. Aged 17.

ISAAC SMIRKED AT me as he stood before me, a long strip of silk twisting through his fingers. I sat on the edge of the bed, completely naked, and looked up at him. Without saying a word, he placed the material over my eyes and pulled it tight into a knot behind my head. Shivering, I reached up to him but he stepped out of my reach.

"Naughty," he whispered in my ear. Goosebumps exploded across my skin with excitement. "You can't touch, birthday girl."

My heart was trying to beat out of my chest when, slowly, he dragged the tip of his finger along my jaw, his tender touch making me turn my face into his caress. But suddenly he yanked my arms behind my back and bound them in another tie.

"You are not to move until I tell you." The tone of his voice was stern as he moved across the room, his voice quietening the further away he got.

The last three months had seen Isaac and me become close. The cold nights after Rogue and Mouse's deaths had hardened me. I was no longer the emotional mess that had threatened to consume me back then. I had become harder on the inside and colder on the outside. I was known as the Cold Bitch in the Phantom residence, and that was fine by me. Frederik, who still punished me for any slight mistake, had also grown to respect me. I was his finest assassin but I figured if he ever found out it was me who had killed Joel then that respect would be lost, only leaving behind his cruelty.

After a while, when I thought Isaac had left me, I jumped when a touch wisped across my breasts. It was feather light, barely decipherable, but it brought my body to life, my skin tingling as I pressed into the stroke. Leisurely, the contact ventured down the front of my body, the back of his fingers lightly brushing against my skin until they started to draw circles on the inside of my thigh. This was so unlike Isaac. He was usually rough and needy, his dominance making his caresses firm and bruising, and although I loved that, the way he was touching me now made my breaths come in small pants.

"Yes," I breathed when those fingers faintly stroked between my wet flesh, the tips tickling my swollen clit. Although the light touch was unbearably delicate, it stimulated something deep inside me and I couldn't hold back the moan when his lips peppered tiny kisses up my inflamed labia.

"You like that?" Isaac whispered in my ear.

I froze as Isaac's voice breathed in my ear and his mouth continued to pleasure my pussy. How could he do that? He didn't have two mouths.

"Isaac?"

"Shh," he encouraged before his mouth crushed my own and he kissed me like his hunger would kill him if he didn't taste me. I groaned into his mouth as the mouth between my legs engulfed my clit with sucks and rapid flicks, my hips writhing uncontrollably as I begged whoever was orally pleasuring me to grant me a climax. When a finger slid inside me and the tip pressed against my front wall, teasing my G-Spot with a slight pressure, I gasped against Isaac's mouth and bit down on his bottom lip, the crushing indulgence of my orgasm driving me into the confinement of pleasure, every muscle in my body locking up with the ecstasy.

Hands pushed me until my back lay against the bed and more hands opened my thighs. A body slid between my legs and when a hard cock thrust inside me I started to panic. "Isaac?"

"It's okay, love, it's me."

Sighing in relief, I started to enjoy the pressure he was building inside me, his fucking growing feverish as his carnal grunts elevated my lust. His cock pounded into me without relief, his punishing pumps making his balls slap against my buttocks as he drove deeper and deeper.

I couldn't hold back my cry when soft lips wrapped around my nipple and a tongue circled the hardness, teeth nipping faintly as they pulled and sucked relentlessly. However they disappeared and Isaac sped up, one hand lifting my backside off the bed so he could drive a couple of fingers into my arse. I was on the edge of falling, my muscles strung so tightly that it was becoming too painful to hold back. Lust controlled me and fierce grunts of need left me as I bucked against my lover with a force that shocked us both. "Fuck me!" I growled. "Harder! Fuck me harder!"

His fingers dug into the flesh of my hips when he did as I asked and banged me with so much vigour that my arms still tied behind my back started to ache.

Suddenly he pulled out of me and flipped me over. Whether he was aware of the strain on my arms or whether he just wanted to take me from behind I wasn't sure but as he slammed back in I felt a movement on the bed above me as Isaac unbound my wrists.

Tensing, but telling myself to go with it, I lifted my face and readied myself for the cock I knew was begging for my mouth. What I didn't expect was to be greeted with a dripping wet pussy.

"What the…"

I yelped when a sharp crack hit my backside. "Eat her!" Isaac demanded.

I didn't know what to do. Isaac was still furiously fucking me, his deep hard drives fuelling my arousal, his fingertips digging into my flesh and encouraging my climax, and his order making me shiver with his dominance. The knowledge that I also had a swollen pussy in my face wasn't dampening my lust either, and confusion floored me when I felt myself lean into the softness. The smell of womanly desire made my belly clench with excitement.

"Eat her, Connie!" Isaac ordered again, his voice tight as he growled through the clench of his jaw. "Put your tongue inside her. Taste her."

His fingers wrapped in my hair and he pushed my face further into the spread of thighs until I gave in and hesitantly drew my tongue up, the taste of femininity blasting over my taste buds. "That's it, my love. Good girl," Isaac said when I stroked my tongue over her clit.

Fingers spread into my hair and a soft gasp told me I was doing something right. Encouraged, I lapped harder, taking the drip of arousal and dragging it down and over her anus.

"Fuck! Fuck!" Becca hissed. The recognition of her voice didn't put me off, instead, now I could picture her, I was eager to make the bitch come for me. There was something about Becca's high estimation of herself that wanted me to make her putty under me. It was hard to explain. As much as I hated her, I wanted to drive her wild with pleasure. I wanted to show her who was boss and that I could make her scream.

Thrusting my fingers inside her, I sucked her clit delicately and manoeuvred my hand until I could press my thumb into her arse. She groaned loudly, pressing her cunt harder into my face.

"Fuck, yes!" Isaac growled as he began to thrust hard and deep inside me. "Fuck her with your fingers, Connie."

I followed his order, my body flying with my own orgasm as Becca broke under me, my fingers driving as deep into her as Isaac was thrusting into me. Erotic moans filled the confines of Isaac's room, each one of us vocalising our orgasms loudly and sensually as the scent of sex permeated the air around us.

Once the arousal had died down, I didn't want to face what had just happened. I couldn't look at Becca as shame heated my cheeks but when Isaac softly undid the blindfold, Becca was nowhere to be seen.

Isaac smiled at me with so much adoration that all my concerns left me immediately, his expression of awe making me smile at him almost shyly.

"You amaze me over and over again." He lifted me onto the bed and curled up beside me, his arms holding me tightly and securely. "Happy birthday, my love." He yawned.

Reality sneaked back in and my mouth dried as I turned to face the man I loved so much. He frowned, sensing my hesitancy. "Is everything okay? Did I hurt you?" When I didn't answer him but stared at him nervously, he cupped my face tenderly. "Shadow?"

Bile filled my mouth and I couldn't help but reach out and touch him. "I..."

"I'm sorry," he whispered frantically. "I shouldn't have done that, I thought..."

"No!" I shook my head, halting his turmoil instantly. "No, I enjoyed it. Although I'm not a Becca lover, I enjoyed it." He chuckled when my cheeks flushed with embarrassment. I'd never seen myself enjoying sex with another woman and I was amazed at how much I'd enjoyed it. However, things were about to get a damn sight more serious and nerves rattled my bones.

"You need to know," I whispered, "that I care for you, Isaac. More than I've ever cared about anyone."

He frowned at me and tensed. "That sounds ominous."

"But I've made up my mind."

"About?"

Dropping my gaze to his chin, I whispered. "I'm having your baby. And I'm keeping it."

My heart shifted into my throat when he stared at me. His eyes didn't widen, nor did they narrow, they just held me captive with a stark coldness. My gut warped as any bile turned to acid. My pulse was raging in my ears, my breathing quickly nearing the stage of hyperventilation.

"Say something," I urged quietly.

But he didn't. Mutely he stood up and walked away. Just walked away.

Chapter Twenty-Four

'Acceptance and hope, that's all we can ever long for.'

BULLET FROWNED AT me when I quietly walked into the kitchen area of West. "Sit down." She pulled out a chair for me when she caught my despair.

Placing a glass of water in front of me, she took the chair beside me and sat patiently waiting until I opened my mouth.

"I'm pregnant," I whispered.

Her gasp was loud but her gaze was so full of pity that I couldn't hold back my tears. "I don't know what to do."

Blowing out a breath, she grabbed my hand and squeezed it. "Well for one, we make sure Frederik doesn't find out."

I lifted both brows at her. "Well that's a given."

"And Isaac?"

Sucking in my lips, I shrugged. "Well, put it this way, he wasn't jumping up and down. How could I have been so stupid? Rule number one... wrap it or don't tap it!"

"Regrets and what ifs are no good now. Acceptance and planning are the only things that will get you through this. Mouse, bless her soul, got caught a couple of years ago. I think I still have the number for the clinic she used."

"What?" I gasped. "Whoa!"

Her expression hardened and her eyes narrowed. "You can't keep it, Shadow."

My heart rate slowed to match each of her syllables, the shock of my announcement slowing each of her horrified words. I knew she was right, a baby couldn't be brought up in this shitpile but hope also blossomed in my belly and dreams flourished in my mind, making anything seem possible. Wiping away a tear, I swallowed my heartache. "But I love it already."

"Shit." She sighed, cupping my face and wiping away a tear with her thumb. "Are you absolutely positive?"

"Yeah." I nodded. "I called into the walk-in clinic in Soho after my last assignment. I'm already fifteen weeks. It's already part of me, Bullet. It's already trusting me to give it life, I can't..." My head shook furiously as my wide eyes begged her. I wanted my best friend to make everything alright, to promise me that I could be a mother, a good mother. But of course she couldn't do that. Yet, promises or not, I swore to my baby that I would do everything I could to keep it safe, as impractical as it seemed right then.

Rubbing her face with her hands, Bullet blew out a breath then nodded firmly. "Then I'll be by your side every step of the way, Shadow. This auntie is gonna have to kick some serious ass, but you know what? Maybe... just – fucking – maybe, girl."

She chuckled at my relieved grin. "Really?"

"You need to stay away from Frederik. You need to follow every damn order to a tee. Keep out of trouble, Shadow. We'll deal with your growing size as we get to it."

"Okay." I nodded, grateful for her taking charge. "Oh by

the way," I added nonchalantly when she got up and headed for the door. "I just had sex with Becca."

The way her feet stumbled was comical, her eyes, full of shocked horror and curiosity, making me giggle. "What the fuck did you just say?"

I nodded slowly and gave her a casual shrug. "Yeah, I had a face full of her pussy."

She dropped back into the chair and gawped at me. "What the fuck?" she repeated.

"A birthday present from Isaac."

She spluttered and swallowed. "Since when did flowers and chocolates go out of fashion?"

"Well, it seems pussy is the in thing this year."

"You hate the bitch!"

Giving her a smile and a wink, I lifted my tired body out of the chair and patted her shoulder. "Yeah, and I made her scream like a fucking banshee."

She blinked at me then the funniest of chuckles resonated from her, forcing free a chuckle of my own. Lifting a hand to me, I high fived her. "Get in, my bitch!"

I was still laughing as I made my way back to my room. I wasn't in it much lately, my nights spent with Isaac, but I had a feeling things would change. His ignorance angered me, but in retrospect, my reaction had been pretty much the same as his. So I was shocked to find him waiting for me in my room with a carrier bag in his hands.

He looked up at me with his sparkling green eyes as his pale face showed each of his worries. His frown seemed deeper, the lines on his forehead more obvious than usual as he chewed his bottom lip with his teeth.

He lifted a hand to me, and hesitantly, I slipped my hand into his. He pulled me to his lap until I had no choice but to part my thighs and drop onto his knee. Dipping his hand into the bag he'd placed on the bed beside him, he pulled out an apple. "Eat," he commanded as he pulled out some cheese. "And this."

I stared at him and took the items. He didn't say anything else as he took more items from the bag. Before long, a pile of food nestled on my bed; kiwis, bananas, oranges, nuts, berries and a whole host of cheeses made my mouth water.

Taking my chin between his finger and thumb, he guided my eyes from the stack to his eyes. "I have to go to Russia for a few weeks. You will eat properly. You will look after yourself. You will be extremely careful around the others. Exercise carefully, train even more carefully. I've given Devlin an order for some vitamins; make sure you take them every day. We want our child to be big and strong."

I couldn't speak as tears flooded my cheeks, my relief and happiness rendering me mute. However, I managed a nod before I took a big bite of the apple, its crisp flavour bursting in my mouth. We weren't afforded fruit as Phantoms, they were considered a luxury. In fact, food was considered a luxury. Food was given when Frederik felt like rewarding us – which wasn't very often.

Isaac laid his hand over my belly. His eyes watered and he blinked to clear his gaze. Framing his face with both my hands I kissed him hard. He moaned into me, his other hand snaking around the back of me to hold me close to him.

"Can we really do this?" I asked timidly, frightened of his answer, but his soft smile made my heart beat that little bit faster with hope.

"I don't know," he answered with a sad sigh. "But damn it, we're gonna try."

"Yeah?"

"Yeah."

And try we would. So fucking hard. But as with everything, your best is never enough. Phantom life was cruel. It didn't just take your life, it took your soul too.

Chapter Twenty-Five

'The best of dreams soon turns to nightmares.'

April 2008.

"IT WAS MY fault," Bullet lied as Frederik held us both before him, Gregory holding me flat to the floor as Jacob pinned Bullet down by her hair.

"What?" I gasped. "No, no, Bullet."

"It was me, Master. I stole it!"

"Bull...." I cried out when Frederik's boot slammed into the side of my hip, the crack loud on contact. I wedged my lips together to stop the scream that wanted to hurtle from my throat.

"Refrain from talking. You are both liars. Liars and whores. I'm holding you both accountable."

Bullet's eyes shot to mine. "I'm sorry," she mouthed. I shook my head at her. I knew why she had done it. I would have taken the blame for her if she was pregnant, knowing what cruel torture Frederik would have lined up for us.

We both flinched when we were pulled up together, both

of Frederik's puppets knowing what he wanted without him having to even voice a command. That's how manipulated we all were.

He walked slowly over to Bullet, his cold eyes making me shiver. He stood before her, looking over her as though she were an insect that had crawled over his food. I hated him so much. I wanted him dead. I wanted to kill him myself, and I think if it weren't for the fact he was my lover's father, I would have ended him by now. I had no doubt in my head I was capable. As Isaac had told me often enough, I was the most formidable Phantom of the whole clan. I also knew this was the only reason Frederik kept me alive, because I was useful to the family, not because of any compassion towards me. If he ever found out about my relationship with his son and heir, then I knew that would change with a snap of his fingers.

I flung forward when Frederik slammed his fist into Bullet's face, knocking her to the ground. Jacob and Gregory grabbed each of my arms, holding me back.

"Master, please don't."

He laughed, shaking his head. "You will see what your disobedience brings, Shadow. You refuse to be controlled. So maybe making your friends take your punishment may start to control you better." He turned back to Bullet. "You stole from me, so I think the only appropriate punishment is to steal something from you."

My eyes remained dry, my ability to cry stripped from me, as my friend took my punishment. They raped her, each of them, after they broke her frail body. One after the other they took her and then all three of them together. My best friend never shed a tear. We held each other's eyes through the duration of our visits to hell. Another piece of my soul shattered as her blood trailed along the ground and pooled against my foot where they had tied me to the pole that was fixed to the floor for occasions of punishment.

Their sick grunts twisted my stomach as Bullet's silence shredded my heart. It was then that I felt my baby kick for the first time. A moment of absolute joy held me up in that moment of sheer desolation. I couldn't close my eyes. I was made to watch what my actions for stealing some bread from the kitchens had brought. We were all so very hungry, each one of us malnourished and weak. It was only because of this that I had managed to hide my pregnancy and I had been amazed at how my baby had survived in the devastating condition my body was in, hence the need to steal food. Unfortunately this time we had been caught as Bullet had kept watch for me.

It was only when a solitary tear leaked from my best friend's eye and trickled across her cheek that the vomit came. "I'm so sorry, Bullet," I whispered. "I'm so, so sorry."

Isaac had been gone for over six weeks and I missed him with my very soul. I'd been hanging from the cross for eight days, the skin on my back hanging off my bulging spinal column after many punishing lashes.

I knew my time to die had come, and in a way, I hungered for it. My soul had perished as the rats had eaten my toes, my own urine providing them with a tasty meal - obviously they were as starved as me. The door to the courtyard had been locked and no one, not even the sentinels were allowed to visit me.

And all because I had refused to slaughter a nine-year-old boy.

He had been my last assignment. And the finality of my life. In the days I swung naked, the rain beating down on me, the icy nights ravaging my frail bones and my arms aching with the weight of my skinny body, all I hoped for was one final smile from Mae and a goodnight kiss from Isaac. That's all I wanted. I didn't pray for food or luxuries. I didn't require extravagant goods or excessive pampering. I just longed for my sister and my lover. I knew Isaac cared for me. He'd never openly expressed it, but I felt it in the way he looked at me, and the way he touched me. And right then, when Frederik walked into the small square area with Panther holding the rain off our Master's head with an umbrella, I knew it was time. And he'd brought my friend to witness my death. That's how sick and mean the bastard was.

Panther gulped as his eyes raked over my dying body, his heartache at the sight of me evident when he squeezed his eyes shut and tried to strengthen himself for the upcoming horror.

"Untie her," Master demanded.

Handing the umbrella to Frederik, Panther stepped forward and yanked at the knots in the rope. "I love you, sister," he whispered as I fell to the ground on my knees, my aching arms unable to support me when I slapped my hands into the mud.

"Get up," Frederik barked.

Attempting to stand, I fell forwards. I considered just laying still, hoping that he would promptly end my suffering for denying his order but pride made me try and when I eventually came to stand before him, the exhaustion debilitated my weary body and I could take no more. I dropped to my knees again, wet mud adding a layer to the dry mud that caked my legs.

I no longer registered the pain, only numbness and an overwhelming need to die.

"Get up," Frederik hissed. I cried out, surprising even myself at the strength my body found to voice my anguish when he brought the whip across my back in punishment. I didn't howl at the agony, only the despair.

"I can't, Master," I managed to croak out, even though my body defied my words and I palmed the ground again to push myself upright. My hand slid in the sludge and I fell forwards, my cheek gliding over the dirt, some of the earth slithering up one of my nostrils. The rain that beat down on me made my skin heavier, making standing even more excruciating. Even the Gods hated me, apparently.

The slurry of dirt picked up by the leather of the whip fed my flesh when my skin split with yet another thrash from my master. "Get up, Shadow!"

Swallowing slowly, I urged myself to stand, the rain laughing at me when its strength mocked me and made the task almost impossible. I didn't care that my bare arse stuck up in the air, I didn't care that blood and mud were now my clothes, I didn't care that my beautiful long black hair had been hacked off, nor did I care that my skin hung off my protruding ribs. The only thing I cared about was my sister, and how my pain and agony gave her peace and happiness. And that in itself gave me the determination to stand once more.

Once I was upright, Frederik walked around me, coming to a halt in front of me. Rain poured from the umbrella Panther held above his head, and cascaded down my face but I knew better than to move from its torrent. I stood still, my eyes blinking furiously as the river lashed over my eyelashes and instinct attempted to close them. I didn't even have the energy to close my mouth as it hung open, the only available input and outpour for air now the mud blocked my nose.

He stepped forward, his foot skidding in the wet earth and his body surging forwards. Panther snatched his hand out and grabbed hold of him. I secretly wished he hadn't done that.

He curled his fingers around my throat and I sagged in his hold, thankful at the support for a brief moment. "What the fuck Isaac sees in you is beyond me. You are weak. A disabled irritant in an existence only for warriors and fighters." His hold on me tightened. I couldn't fight him anymore, I didn't have the energy. I wanted to die; I craved for it.

I dropped to the ground when he opened his hand, screaming at the pain that erupted through my kneecaps when they smashed on the concrete below the cross. I knew I had shattered one, my malnutrition made them brittle and fragile. The agony made my body jerk and vomit spew from my belly. I was surprised there was anything to throw up. I hadn't eaten for days and I was concerned it was my stomach lining that had torn away when a spray of blood coated Frederik's legs.

He tutted, his cold stare locking on what painted him. My body instinctively curled in on itself when the heel of his boot slammed into my stomach. I had thought the pain before that had been unbearable but this was something altogether worse. Yet it wasn't the pain from his kick that ripped my soul from me, it was the fact that I knew his cruelness had just killed the tiny person that was growing inside me.

A wail shattered the air around us when I immediately felt the warm rush between my legs, the torturous sound only a mother losing her child could make.

"What the hell?" Frederik barked when his eyes dropped to the rush of blood flowing over my thighs.

"No!" His scream was both agonising and welcoming. My eyes lifted in time to see Isaac race from the house and plunge the knife straight through Frederik's gut, his rage twisting it cruelly, his wrath dragging it back out so he could stab the bastard in the heart over and over again.

Frederik's body dropped beside me, his dead open eyes fixed on me. Blood trickled from the corner of his mouth and merged with my own.

"No!" Isaac wailed as he lifted me gently in his arms. Panther stood, his mouth agape, his eyes wide and flicking between Frederik and Isaac. "Contact the medic, and have her meet me in the infirmary!" Isaac barked as he rushed through the courtyard with me. "Panther!"

The world was leaving me, heaven closing in, the angels tempting me with serenity as they welcomed my baby into their arms.

"Stay with me, my love. Don't you dare close those beautiful eyes," Isaac whispered as he ran. "Look at me, Connie." The fact that he used my name made me slowly open my eyes.

His feet slipped in the wet mud but he kept going, his vigour and strength the only thing keeping me from death. "I'm going to fix you, I promise. I'm going to fix this." He lifted his hand to my face, his power and my frailty allowing him to carry me with one arm whilst he continued to move fluidly through the house. "I love you," he stated matter-of-factly. "I love you, Connie. We'll get through this. I promise."

I stared at him. Using what little energy I had left, I lifted my own hand slowly to his handsome face. I didn't have the ability to voice my own declaration but as I pressed my hand into his wet cheek, I managed a faint smile.

He sucked on his lips, his despair showing a side to him I had never seen. The death of our child not only gutted him, but gave him the strength to voice his emotions. Isaac didn't ever allow his feelings to control him, yet in that moment, he understood as did I, that any hope I had ever had of having children had been snatched from me. And I would never be the same girl again.

Hardness overtook my heart. Detachment overruled my spirit. And grief tortured my soul as I slipped away from the cruel world and begged for peace as the darkness welcomed me.

Chapter Twenty-Six

*'We move forward, we move on.
But we will never forget.'*

Isaac

IT HAD BEEN ten days since my child and my father had died within minutes of each other. Grief couldn't overpower the feeling of uselessness inside me when, upon hunting for Connie after she'd been released from the infirmary, I found her knelt at the cross, her gaze fixed on the place our baby had died.

"Hey." I spoke quietly as I went to sit beside her.

She was so pale, the toll of the last month showing so evidently on her broken skin. She'd lost so much weight, but more than that, she'd lost her spirit and that was the very thing that broke me too. I'd been sorting things with Artur in Russia, reporting back to him my findings over the last six months. He'd finally given me the go ahead to terminate my father's rule, but as usual I had been too late. Just ten minutes earlier and I could have saved our baby.

Connie blinked slowly at me, the sadness in her eyes making my gut tighten. "I can't do this anymore, Isaac. I don't want to. I want to go with her."

"Her?"

Instinctively, she nuzzled into my touch when I placed my palm against her face. "Isabella Mae," she whispered.

The lump in my throat and heart was proving too difficult to breathe through and I swallowed in attempt to relieve the pressure. "We were having a girl?"

She nodded, dropping her gaze to the brown patch that offered a memorial for our daughter. "Yes. Valerie scanned me secretly a couple of weeks ago." Valerie was the nurse in the Phantom infirmary. I made a mental note to praise her for keeping our secret.

Shuffling around so my body was in front of her I grabbed her hands in my own. "It's over Connie. Frederik is gone."

She smiled but it was so full of sorrow. "It will never be over, Isaac. I've lost my sister, my parents, my friends and now my daughter. They will never set me free from the ache inside. And to be honest, I don't want to be set free. I want to feel this anger, this pain because it makes them real, it keeps them alive. But I'm not sure I can live with the agony either. It's torturous."

Her head fell forwards and she rested her forehead against mine. Tears dripped from her eyes, her sparkling blues now a mere dull grey as her soul wept with her and revealed to me its turmoil. "Please, Isaac."

I frowned, not grasping what she was asking. "Anything. I'll do anything but I don't know what to do, Connie."

"I want you to end it for me."

My heart dropped into my stomach and I reared back. Unthinking, I hit out and slapped her hard across her pale cheek. The blood rushed to the surface, tinting her whiteness rosy red as she crumpled before me and the most horrific wail tore from her as her grief burst to the surface. "Please," she begged. "I want to go. I'm so tired. I'm afraid of being afraid, Isaac. I don't want to breathe anymore…"

"Connie!" She whimpered at my stern growl. "You know I would do anything for you. Anything. But I will never, *never*, allow you to leave me."

Her mouth fell open as her eyes widened. "What?"

I shook my head in frustration. "I love you, damn it. You, you're the only thing that keeps me breathing. I can't do this shit without you. I'm the master now, Connie. And damn it, I need you with me. I need you to hold me up when it all sinks to shit. I need you to keep me warm at night. I need your body to pleasure mine. And I need you beside me, keeping the Phantoms going."

She blinked at me before her eyes widened in shock. "What are you saying?"

"I'm saying it's about time you became Mrs Connie Marinov." She froze, her eyes growing larger by the second, her mouth falling farther open the more I stared her out. She gulped loudly when I ran my finger delicately along her lip. "No one will ever hurt you again. Shadow is a Phantom. But you, Connie Swift, are mine, to have and to hold, for richer, for poorer, in sickness and in…"

I groaned when she crushed her mouth to mine, her sob echoing into my mouth as her tongue fought for the comfort of mine. Her tiny hands grabbed at my hair as her passionate assault stole both our breaths.

"I love you," she whispered when she broke away.

And she did. So very much. Nearly as much as I loved her.

The Beginning of *Connie & Isaac*

We married on the 7th May, 2008. Connie wore a bright red dress, her new short hair pinned back with tiny diamond pins. She looked stunning and her smile was the only thing that got me through the formality of the day.

We were happy, so very happy. Our sex life went from strength to strength, both of us enjoying various partners as we both needed the escape of a varied sex life. But as much as we fucked others, we were never intimate with anyone other than each other.

I ruled the Phantoms with a stern control, but I considered myself fair. No longer did we kidnap and torture soldiers into becoming something they didn't want. We only took on those that wanted to be with us, those who wanted to earn good money while they each took contracts they wanted. Although some rules I kept in place to keep the establishment running smoothly, torture no longer became a part of training. We refused to hurt anyone under the age of eighteen, and if a contract came in where it required just that, then the child would be given a new identity and adopted out to homes that went through thorough checks by specialists. The government, the police force and even the army all accepted our existence, after all, the Phantoms on a few occasions helped out with matters that they felt were a little too delicate for them to be associated with.

We all lived happily ever after.

Then, in March 2013, a month after her twenty-second birthday, Connie learned of her sister's death. And our lives changed forever.

PART III

Chapter Twenty-Seven

'Hope is the life we think we lost.'

Connie

March 2013. Aged 22.

THE MIST APPEARED to be crawling towards me. I didn't move, refusing to let it push me away. I'd been pushed away too many times and I wouldn't allow anyone or anything to do it again.

My heart ached as I stood under the cover of the trees, their heavily laden branches providing a secluded hideaway as I watched the small congregation gather by the graveside. A couple of people opened umbrellas when the rain began to fall heavier, immediately dampening down the curling fog.

I recognised most of them. I was surprised Tammy had come; she'd always bullied Mae at school. And Bonnie, another two-faced bitch my sister and I had avoided like the plague.

I swiped at the tears that flooded down my cheeks. A part of me had gone, evaporated from inside me. My soul felt incomplete, my heart had split down the middle.

I couldn't decipher what the vicar was saying from so far away but I didn't need his words. They wouldn't comfort me, nor would they take away the ache or the guilt. Bonnie wailed when the vicar threw a lump of soil on top of Mae. What the fuck? Dramatic skank.

My eyes widened when a tall, dark-haired man stepped out from behind a woman with a large umbrella. I hadn't noticed him before, and from the sheer size of him I wondered why. His long black coat was drenched, his dark brown hair slicked across his forehead as streams of rain ran down his face. I could see the drops dripping from his long eyelashes even from the distance between us.

He stood by the edge of the hole, looking down into it with a severe frown. He looked angry; angry at Mae for dying, possibly. I understood because I felt it too. The rage that had engulfed me when one of my contacts notified me of her death had been the most unreal feeling I had ever felt, even greater than the grief of losing my parents… or rather my mother.

I cocked my head in puzzlement when he dropped a single deep red rose onto her coffin. His fists clenched before he brought one up to his lips and kissed it then tossed something else into the grave.

Loud sobs filtered across the cemetery, the driving rain doing nothing to stop the weeping as people wandered off.

Waiting until everyone had left, I trudged across the muddy ground and stopped beside my sister's final resting place.

"Hey," I whispered as I brought my gaze down to the

wooden box that held Mae. A deep tightening in my chest brought on a gasp of pain and I closed my eyes for a moment. The rain beat down on me, punishing me for the sins I had committed against my own flesh and blood. "I'm so sorry, Mae."

The silence tore at me until the pain became too much and I stepped back to leave. A splash of white from the coffin caught my attention. It was obviously what the tall guy had thrown in. I squinted, trying to focus on what it was but I couldn't make it out.

Pulling my phone from my inside pocket, I quickly snapped a shot of the object. Opening up the camera album, I swiped at the screen as the rain beaded, distorting the image before I zoomed in and stared in shock.

I stumbled backwards, losing my footing, my heart thudding loudly in my ears, and my arse landing in the mud when a two-year-old *us* stared back at me. However, this wasn't one of us, this was the essence of Mae. It was a new photo, the clothes the child wore were modern. She was sitting on the bonnet of a car, smiling widely for the shot. Her long black hair was in pigtails, and her bright blue eyes - Mae's eyes, my eyes - twinkled brightly. This year's registration on the car confirmed my thoughts.

Holy fuck.

Mae had a family. I had a niece. And the guy who had dropped in the photo was obviously her husband.

My heart burst for her, my sorrow lifting before intensifying when the reality of what she had to leave behind consumed me. She had found the very thing she had always wanted. Relief coursed through me, any taste of happiness she could have lived before passing should be celebrated. I thought I had broken her when I… when I left. Thought I had given her more of a reason to want to leave this dismal place and join our parents. And the fact that she was now with *him* agonised me.

He shouldn't be granted time with his daughter in the afterlife, he didn't deserve that. The only hope I held onto was that the devil had claimed his rotten soul, and refused him sanctuary with my mother and sister.

I brushed my thumb over the happy picture, saving it to my phone as wallpaper and smiled. I wasn't alone anymore. There wasn't only me that remained of the Swift family.

I needed to find them, both her and Mae's husband.

But it turned out that he wasn't Mae's husband. He wasn't even her lover. It was over the following months that I found out exactly who Daniel Shepherd really was.

And exactly who I was.

Chapter Twenty-Eight

'Knowledge can be painful.'

November 2013.

BULLET CURLED UP in my bed yet again and I sighed sadly and cuddled her to me. "You okay, sister?"

She remained silent but nodded. My heart went out to my best friend. She'd been in love with Panther for years and as much as I encouraged her to tell him, she refused. Isaac had thrown another famous Phantom party, and after battling with an excruciating headache all day, I was hiding away in my room. Although Isaac and I were married, we still had our own separate rooms where we could just relax and be ourselves. I loved Isaac, I did, but I was still very much isolated in my own life. We shared rings, we shared bodies and sometimes, occasionally, we shared thoughts but aside from that, we were still our own people. And it suited us both.

"Panther got a friend over for the night again?"

She turned into me, burying her face into my chest as she

broke out into a sob. "I want to stab her," she growled.

"Who?"

"Whoever the skank is in his fucking bed."

"Bullet just tell him, for Christ's sake. You never know…"

"No!" She shook her head firmly. "I have to work with him, Shadow. If he knows how I feel about him it will compromise all our…"

"I have to go away for a while," I cut in. I'd been dreading telling her and for some strange reason I found blurting it out in the middle of her sentence easier to do.

Her eyes lifted to me as she pulled back so she could see the whole of my face. "Is this to do with Annie?"

She shifted away from me and I sat up, opening the drawer beside my bed to pull out the bottle of vodka. Bullet grabbed the two glasses I kept on the dresser for our nightly moans and encouraged me to fill them to the brim before we both rested back against the wall. "Annie has been marked."

"What the fuck?" Bullet gasped, choking down a mouthful of Grey Goose.

"Her and… *daddy*." The way I spat 'daddy' made Bullet smirk.

"I take it you and the notorious Mr Shepherd are going to have some fun."

The chuckle that broke from me was as cold as my feelings towards Mae's torturer. "Oh, I plan on having lots of fun with him. But first I have to get Annie to feel safe with me. Isaac has already prepared her a family for when it's over."

Bullet sighed and looked at me curiously. "And Isaac's okay with this?"

"With what?"

"With you being so close to the target. I'm surprised he's sanctioned your involvement to be honest."

When she noticed me tense, she narrowed her eyes and tipped her head. "He has sanctioned your involvement?"

"Of course he has," I said carefully.

But my best friend knew me better than anyone and she growled. "For fuck's sake, Shadow. What the hell are you doing?"

"He has!" I defended but then sighed. "He's planning on moving my niece abroad, Bullet. She's my niece. The only family we have is each other. I can't allow that. She's my sister's baby, my flesh and blood."

"Shadow…"

"No! I'm going in there and I'm going to end that bastard, and if needs be I will go into hiding with Annie. She's mine, Bullet and even Isaac won't take her from me."

"Oh, my friend." Bullet sighed as she gripped my hand tightly. "She's not Isabella…"

"Fuck you!" I spat out, glaring at her as I scurried off the bed. "Fuck you! Don't you think I don't know that? I do! I know that, but she is Mae's and I will sign myself over to the devil to love that little girl!"

She stared after me, shouting my name as I slammed my own room door behind me and tore through the Phantom mansion. I knew she wasn't Isabella. Annie was Mae's daughter, I wasn't deluded. Yet, I was her auntie and that bastard who she lived with didn't deserve her. He deserved to feel the edge of my blade across his throat, and by fucking God was he going to feel it.

The hatred of what he did to Mae consumed me yet again, and I palmed the wall in attempt to control my raging breaths. My belly curdled with fury, my mouth watering as I pictured what I was going to do to Daniel Shepherd. Rage engulfed me, my heart beating furiously as I struggled to contain my emotions.

I needed Isaac, he was the only person who could ground me, who could snap me out of my shit and make me understand what was real and what hope could bring me.

His quarters, or rather our marital suite, was quiet when I quietly slipped inside. Curling my lip at the thought of him entertaining, or in simple terms 'fucking' someone, I blew out a breath and hesitantly popped my head around his bedroom door. Frowning to myself when I found it empty, I pouted. I needed his arms around me. I needed his soft words in my ear to stop the ache that was constant inside me, to put it to rest just for ten minutes.

A noise in the bathroom halted me just as I was about to leave. Cautiously opening the door and hoping he wasn't having a number two, I stepped inside.

Now, before I go on, I need you to understand mine and Isaac's relationship. We loved each other, there was no doubt about that. Yet we were both very sexual creatures. Sex, to both of us, wasn't sentimental or intimate, it was a way of releasing stress and receiving pleasure. As much as a massage, an expensive bottle of wine or a luxurious hot bath can to you be pleasurable, fucking to us was very much on the same level. Our bodies weren't our souls and our hearts weren't connected to our genitals. Love was very much emotions and feelings, whereas sex was purely physical, it was quite simple to us. We were created to procreate, it was only religion that brought marriage into the equation and as such, to Isaac and me anyway, sex and love were on completely different parallels. We weren't jealous, in fact we often told each other about other partners as we lay wrapped in each other's arms at night. It not only widened our own minds but it gave us new things to explore. However, what we never shared with others was our mouths or our hearts. My lips and my heart belonged to Isaac and vice versa. Those things were personal, something that connected us to our innermost feelings. A kiss, for example, wasn't pleasurable in the way fucking can be. We didn't kiss to orgasm, we kissed because we needed that closeness to the other person. To share breaths is to share hearts and if my heart only beat for Isaac, then my breath should only be shared with him. I hope all that makes sense and you can gain a little more understanding to how we both were before I tell you the next part of our tale.

The bathroom was relatively light, the main lamp lit. No music played or candles burned; there was nothing remotely romantic in the situation but my heart clenched when I found my husband bathing my fucking nemesis.

Both Isaac and Becca looked up at me as Isaac sponged the bitch down. I blinked at them both, desperately trying to hang on to my sanity.

"Hey, love." Isaac smiled up at me as though nothing unusual was happening. Becca grinned at me with a frosty smirk on her cruel lips and I stood there, completely still as my eyes raked over their naked bodies.

My teeth snapped together. Isaac saw it before she did and just as he moved quickly, I was faster. Whipping the bitch up by her hair, I dragged her out of the bath and hauled her perfect tight arse out of my home, her gasp loud when I threw her out of the door.

Spinning around when I slammed shut the front door, I saw Isaac standing with narrow eyes, ready for me. He ducked – unfortunately – when I picked up a solid brass ugly fucking ornament and launched it at his head. "You bastard!"

I screamed at him. "You fucking bastard!"

"What the fuck, Con? What have I…?"

"I've had the shittiest day!" I bellowed at him. "All I wanted was my husband's arms and I find you intimate with that… that fucking skank!"

"Intimate? We were having a fucking bath!"

"Exactly!" I cried as I propelled the fruit bowl at him, the bananas bouncing off the wall and hitting him, quite brilliantly, in the face. "A bath is not what we would term pleasurable. It's intimate!"

He screwed up his face and swatted away a couple of apples as he stared at me with confusion. "Is it? It's a bath. I was mucky, and she wanted to give me a blowjob." He shrugged as though that explained everything, which in effect it did, but it still didn't satisfy my rage.

"Well why didn't you bathe alone? Why did she have to join you?"

Sometimes I swear men are created with completely different brains than females. He peered at me like I was crazy, "She joined me so she could suck my cock while I was washing. It saved on time… and effort. What's the big deal?" He was growing angry with me but that didn't dampen my own temper.

"You bloody twat," I spat as I hit out at him with my hands, saving the furnishings. "Why her! Why that fucking slag?"

His rage snapping, he grabbed my wrists to stop my assault and pushed me until my back hit the long table that sat along one wall of the hallway. "Will you stop!" he growled. "You fuck Devlin! What's the difference?"

"The difference is he doesn't fucking bathe with me, you arsehole!"

His lip curled and he snarled before he spun me around and pressed my face down on the table, his firm grip on the back of my neck unforgiving and painful. I yelped when he yanked down my jeans and struck my backside harshly. "You need to remember who the fuck you're talking to. Show some fucking respect!"

"Respect!" I scoffed as I fought back, but he was stronger than me and as fast as I managed to get up, he had me back down, my body bent over the table as he tore at my jeans. "Respect is earned!"

"Oh, fuck off, you sulky bitch!" he shouted as he thrust his cock deep inside me.

"Get the fuck off me!" I cried out, bucking back on him as pleasure curled through my angry bones.

"Yeah?" he spat out as he grabbed a fistful of my hair. "Tell me you don't want my big cock inside that tight fucking cunt of yours? Tell me!" he shouted as he pounded into me so hard the edge of the table cut into my belly.

Bouncing back on every one of his drives inside me, I couldn't tell him. "Fuck you, you bastard."

He laughed coldly as he sank his thumb inside my anus and pushed hard. "Look at you, you fucking love it, don't you? Such a greedy wife," he grated through his tight jaw. "Your little pussy drips for me and my cock. You hunger for it!"

My body hovered on the edge of heaven as he fucked me like an animal, each of his cruel pushes inside me lifting me higher and higher. His teeth sank into my neck as he bent over me, his cock screwing harder and deeper. I shivered when I felt my skin burst in his mouth and my blood coated his lips. "Kiss me, bitch," he demanded as he snatched my chin and turned my face to his then slammed his lips on mine and pushed his tongue into my mouth. I could taste my own blood but it only fired the heat in my gut.

He groaned into me as he bucked and jerked, his cum spilling inside me and detonating my own fierce orgasm as I screamed at the constriction of every muscle in my taut body. All the tension left me almost instantly and I sagged into his arms when he pulled me up and took me into his arms, carrying us both through to the bedroom where he lay me on the bed and settled beside me.

"Better?" he asked as he placed a gentle kiss in my hair.

Nodding, I sighed and snuggled against him. "Don't do that again."

"You know Becca is nothing more to me than a cunt, my love. Why do you do this?"

I shrugged, hating all the emotional shit that was burying my heartbeat. "Just not Becca. I know how she feels about you, and she loves it when she brags in South about bedding you. You should hear the skank, she fucking preens…"

"Well, can't you blame her, she has had the master of cocks, Connie. Who wouldn't brag?"

I slapped at him playfully but when I sighed, he tilted my chin back and gazed at me. "Okay, if it means that much to you, no more Becca."

"Thank you," I whispered, giving him a wide smile. "And no more baths."

He pursed his lips considering my request. "Well I might start to smell…"

"You know what I mean," I grumbled. "Just have them on your own, or with me. It's intimate, Isaac. Whatever you say to argue that fact, it's important to me."

His expression changed to one of seriousness and adoration and he nodded. "Okay, I promise. Baths are intimate and not cool."

Little did I know, not a year later I would share a bath with another man. A man I had sworn to kill. A man that I had set out to hate, and ended up loving. And it was that very bath that made me re-evaluate everything in my life.

The next day, I started my very last assignment. It would see many finalities in my life and the beginning of many others, and the start of mine and Isaac's marriage in a way. Daniel Shepherd taught me many things but most of all he taught me about myself.

And for that I would forever be in his debt.

Chapter Twenty-Nine

'And finally, in salvation we find redemption.'

August 2014. Aged 23.

HELEN ACTUALLY OPENED the front door to us when Isaac and I pulled into the thin gravel driveway. Isaac quirked an eyebrow at me before pulling the car up to a stop in front of the door.

"Well, she looks full of the joys of spring," he mocked when Helen stared at us with a bored expression.

"Mmm," I agreed, sighing heavily.

"She looks delightful." His lip curled when his gaze roved down her body then back up to her stern face. "How would you like to do this, my love? Quick or slow?"

Stifling a yawn, I rolled my head round my shoulders. "Fast and easy. I just want a hot bubble bath, a foot rub and your tongue in my pussy." It had been a long eighteen months and I was tired. I'd missed my husband with my very soul and after everything that had happened with Daniel and me, it made me realise just how much I loved Isaac.

Isaac snatched up his gun and grabbed the door handle. I laughed, holding his arm and pushing the gun back onto his lap. "Whoa, stud. Slow down. We have to think of Annie."

"Well hurry. I need you. I've been on rations."

I gawped at him, my mouth wide with shock. "What?"

He shrugged, almost embarrassed as his eyes lowered to his lap. "They're not you, Connie. They never have been. And to be honest, they bore me. My wife, well, she excites me. She makes me laugh in the bedroom. She even breaks wind when I tickle her." He nodded slowly as though proud of my ability to fart. "She makes my cock feel absolutely fucking fantastic but more than that, she loves me, she adores me. And I've realised after all this time, that's what makes it what it is with you. Your love, and my love for you. And there is no greater climax than coming deep inside of you as your eyes give me all your thoughts, your soul and your heart. That's what makes me yours, and that's what makes us fucking awesome in bed." He ran his fingertip across my cheekbone, collecting the tears that fell. "Are you ready?"

"I need to do this on my own."

He smiled, nodding. "I'll come in and get the munchkin, then she's all yours."

"Are you sure you want to do this?" I asked as I looked in his eyes. He shook his head in confusion. "Annie. Bringing Annie into our family."

"My love, Annie is already in our family. She has been ever since she was born. She's part of you, and that makes her part of us. I want her to have that puppy, and days on the beach, and water fights. I want to make her laugh, I want to tickle her until she can't breathe. And I want to watch her pick up her first ever baby and sing to her. I want to be the one who walks her down the aisle when she falls in love, I want to shoot at the prick that breaks her heart and I want her to grant me a grandbaby. Because she's part of *you*, Connie."

"You know," I whispered, unable to lift my voice higher with the emotion coursing through me. "An hour ago, I was regretting what life had given me. But I'd do it all again, three thousand times over, because it gave me you. I look at Mae's life, and yes, although it was my choices that gave her hers, she had to wait until death to find what I've had since I was thirteen. And that gives me cause to be grateful. I have never known a man love a woman as much as you love me. You went against the rules and took the most severe punishment for me. You killed your father for me. But above all that, you love me. Me, the ordinary girl who had to make a choice on a dark winter's night. A choice that changed everything. But take me back there right now and I would make that same choice."

"Will you stop," he whined. "I'm seriously thinking about making love to you now." His brows furrowed. "You know, like... slowly and softly." He stared at me in shock with himself.

"We could try," I whispered.

His pursed his lips in thought. "You mean, no spanking, no belt, no yanking your hair? Just...."

"Just us."

He leaned into me, his warm breath whispering over me as he slid his fingers around the side of my neck. "I'd love to."

I beamed at him before flicking my eyes to an even more bored Helen. Her arms were crossed across her chest while she waited for us. I blew out a breath and opened the door.

"Let's do this. Let's go fetch our little person and finish it."

"I'm right behind you, my love. For the very last time, Shadow." He nodded seriously, giving me the courage I needed to do this.

Closing my eyes briefly, I pulled in a fortifying breath. "Time to reach the end square."

Everyone cooed over Annie when Isaac and I walked into the Phantom house with her. Her own beautiful blue eyes were wide and soaking everything up. Bullet grinned at me, her eyes full of tears as she bobbed down in front of Annie, who was currently holding Isaac's hand so hard I thought she would crush his fingers. "Hello, Annie," she said gently. "My name is Bullet, but you would make me really happy if you called me Elle."

"Elle," Annie whispered as if trying out the sound of Bullet's real name.

"I'm your Auntie Shad...Connie's best friend." I couldn't help but smile when I spotted Panther's hand in my friend's, even as she bent down to talk to Annie. "And I hope me and you are going to be the best of friends too."

Annie nodded and smiled as she timidly looked at all the Phantoms who came to say hello one by one. She was overwhelmed and maybe a little confused by such a large family. But as I looked at my friends, and the love and support they were already giving my niece, I knew deep in my heart that she would never be short of an auntie or uncle, and that they would protect her with their lives. What four-year-old could say that?

Once, a long time ago, I'd hated this life. I'd wanted to end it, I'd wanted to join Mae and leave this shit behind. But now I couldn't ever imagine life without my family.

Surprisingly, Becca sidled up to me and smiled bashfully. "Good to have you back, Shadow."

I frowned at her, trying to peer into her soul to find what cruel joke she had up her sleeve but she blushed and lowered her eyes to the floor like a chastised six-year-old. "I know me and you haven't exactly ever hit it off," she admitted quietly. "But," she licked her lips nervously and smiled with so much tenderness at Annie that I had to blink to stop my eyes from widening in shock. "But I would really like to be a part of your niece's life. We all know this life takes away our chances of having children, and that's a shame. But Annie here, maybe she can be the little person we all want, and need, in our lives."

Weighing up her words, I looked around the room, and my heart clenched in pain when I took in all the smiling and clucking women. They all regarded Annie as some sort of God, their praises and attention to her making me sigh with sadness.

"You know what, Becca?" I spoke loudly. "The Phantoms are a family. Why the hell can't you have a kid if you want one?"

A couple of women stared at me as if I'd ordered them to strip naked and do the hokey-cokey. "Are you serious, Shadow?" Princess, a fairly new assassin who got her tag because of her love of diamonds, asked.

Isaac stepped up beside me after leaving Bullet to scoop Annie into her arms and introduce her to all her new family. Taking my hand in his, he addressed the others. "I have a few things to clear up. For one, no one has ever come to me asking to extend our family. I'm not sure why you all think this is beyond the rules. As Connie said, we are a family. We take care of each other and that includes each other's children. Two," he continued as everyone turned to respectfully listen to their master, "Shadow is now to be addressed by her name. Her proper name." I couldn't help but smile at the warm feeling inside as Isaac squeezed my hand. "And three." He paused and looked to Devlin, who frowned and looked rather nervous. Isaac took a big breath and looked back to the crowd. "Connie and I are retiring."

A range of gasps rang out and every single wide eye stared at Isaac in shock as a few hushed whispers reverberated around the room.

"Devlin will be your new master."

Devlin's eyes grew so wide I swore they were going to pop out and drop at his feet. "Are you shitting me?"

Isaac shook his head. "You have shown me more loyalty than any fucker ever has. Although I'll still be overseeing things from wherever Connie, Annie and I end up, things will very much be left in your rule. I trust you. You've served the Phantoms and me well and I love you for your astounding support."

Devlin smirked but his expression showed every bit of his growing astonishment. "You love me? Wow, I must say I'm honoured."

"Fuck off!" Isaac grumbled, but grinned and pulled Devlin into a hug when he came over and slapped Isaac respectfully on the back.

"Connie," Annie whispered as she nervously came to me and tugged on my hand.

Smiling down at her, I crouched and tucked a loose strand

of her hair behind her ear. "What's wrong, sweetie?"

She leaned into my ear, her cheeks tinted pink with shyness around the others. "Where's my daddy?"

Grief twisted my gut and for a long moment I stared at her in frozen numbness. Tears filled my eyes as I looked at her wide pleading eyes. My mouth dried and it fell open and closed many times before Isaac came to rescue me.

Scooping Annie up into his arms, he smiled at her. "Connie and I need to show you your new room. I think you're going to love it, munchkin."

Isaac looked over at me, his expression full of pity yet his love giving me so much strength. "You ready to do this?"

For over ten years I had been tortured and had tortured. I had killed and been killed many times over. I had put bullets into many people, I had even received a few myself. I had fought with my bare hands, I'd been whipped to within an inch of my life. Yet, right then, I knew the job I now had to face was going to be the most painful thing I had ever undertaken.

Blowing out a breath to calm my anguish, I nodded then silently followed Isaac through the mansion to the north wing. I'd been gone for eighteen months but my things, my home comforts all welcomed me back as though I had never left. My own belongings eased the rage in my heart and gave me the strength to face what I had to do.

Annie climbed into my lap when Isaac sat beside me on the sofa. Her eager expression tormented my soul and when a sob finally broke from me, Isaac smiled sadly.

I watched in stunned silence when he pulled a dice from his pocket and handed it to Annie. She peered at it curiously as she turned it around in her fingers and my despair grew when I realised Isaac had kept the thing that had both granted me death and saved my life.

"You see this?" he whispered as he took Annie's tiny hand in his own. "This belonged to your very brave daddy."

"It's okay," I cut in. "I can do this."

"Are you sure?" he whispered softly as he wiped away one of my tears with his thumb.

Nodding, I turned to Annie. Taking the dice from her hand, I softly rolled it between my fingers. "Your daddy saved my life, Annie."

"He did?" Annie beamed at me. She had the most amazing smile and for a moment I could only stare at the mirror image of my beautiful sister. How fucking cruel was life? How bitter and sick was the person who decided who lived and died? I made a promise that day, that if anyone ever hurt this little girl again, I would annihilate them until all that was left was the dust from their despicable souls.

I nodded, smiling at her through the tears threatening to strangle me. "Do you know how much your daddy loved your mummy, Annie?"

"Lots and lots and lots," she answered eagerly.

"He did," I confirmed with a nod. "And your daddy missed your mummy so, so much, his heart hurt without her."

Blowing out a breath I squeezed her hand so tight I was worried I was hurting her. "Well, the angels came and asked him if he wanted to be with her."

Her eyes filled with huge drops of grief. She understood what I was trying to tell her. A long, piercing whine burst from her lips and she buried her face into my chest as her little fat fingers clawed at my clothes. The look of utter desolation on Isaac's face will forever be etched into my heart when he heard the wretched sound that broke from Annie that day. It will forever fuel my nightmares, and for the first time ever,

I watched as a tear slid down Isaac's face and dropped from his chin onto his strong chest.

"But he loves me too," Annie sobbed.

Oh dear God.

"He loved you so very much, Annie, don't you ever think he didn't. He also loved me too." Isaac tipped his head to the side and regarded me softly. "And he knew how much I longed for a little girl to love. He gave us both a gift when he went to live with your mummy. Everything is so hard right now, but when you're much bigger and your heart doesn't hurt as much as it does now, then things will be easier to understand. But I can promise you that Isaac and I love you with every single piece of our hearts. Your mummy and daddy will always be with you, sweetie, always. Their souls will both comfort and protect you every day."

"Is he happy now?" she whispered.

"He was happy, Annie…"

She shook her head but smiled. "Whenever we went to visit Mummy's grave he would be so sad that it made my tummy hurt. He had a photo of her in his drawer beside his bed…"

I smiled through the pain threatening to rip my heart from my chest. "He's happy, baby. And he wants you to be happy. And I promise you that you will be. I promise Annie," I swore as I wrapped a strand of her hair around my finger and tugged it gently.

She nodded, snuggling into me again. I looked up at Isaac who was staring at me curiously. His expression was soft, his head cocked to one side as he regarded us like some priceless artefact. Reaching out slowly, he took a piece of my hair and a lock of Annie's matching ebony strands and wrapped them both around his little finger. "My girls," he whispered. "My family."

Turning in my hold, Annie smiled at him. "I like you," she said shyly.

I couldn't help but chuckle when the grin that covered Isaac's usual stern face broke all records and his happiness with her statement made my own smile hurt my cheeks.

I knew he longed for a child of his own. The loss of our daughter had hardened Isaac in so many ways, and it was in that single moment that a four-year-old girl managed to smash through the ice that had formed around his heart and annihilate all the hatred he had held for so long.

Annie was the start of living for Isaac and me. She allowed us to breathe and, for the first time ever, to take life and enjoy it. In the years to come, Annie always said that Isaac and I were her saviours, but she was so very wrong. Because she saved us, in so many ways. She was the first proper beat of our hearts, and she was the obliteration to the hatred we both held.

She was our decimation, our salvation and our beginning.

Epilogue

*'If we pray hard enough, we may one day
be granted our hopes and dreams.'*

Isaac

July 2015. Aged 30.

THE SUN BEAT down on my bare chest. Sweat poured from my brow. My muscles had never ached so much. And I had never laughed as damn hard as I was right then.

Both of my girls squealed in delight when I tore after them, the sand whipping up behind me as I ran. They each wore red bathing suits, and they were the prettiest girls on the whole beach.

Annie looked over her shoulder, trying to see how far behind I was. When she spotted me hot on her tail, she screamed and forced her little legs to move faster.

"You'll never escape!" I roared.

"You big mean Toad King!" Annie grumbled when I scooped her up, slung her over my shoulder and raced after Connie who had managed to gain some distance.

"The Toad King is gonna gobble you up, little girl!"

She beat playfully at my back, her tiny fists pounding at my flesh. I was secretly proud of how hard she could already punch. My girl was going to annihilate any fucking boy that came near her. Her little legs kicked, her heel catching me in the eye and blinding me for a brief moment. "Shit," I cried out as I dropped her and pressed the heel of my hand into my throbbing eyeball.

She stared up at me, a delighted grin on her face, before she took the opportunity to escape and belted after Connie. "Traitor!" I shouted after her when Connie laughed loudly upon witnessing her niece's no holds barred fighting skills.

"Good girl!" Connie high-fived Annie and pulled her into her arms as they both made their way down to the crystal clear waters of St Lucia.

"Run!" Bullet shouted to Connie and Annie as she lay curled in Panther's arms. Vaulting over their lazy arses, I scowled at Bullet on my way past. She poked her tongue out and then disappeared under Panther's body when he rolled her very pregnant body over and stuck his tongue in her mouth.

"You're too fat!" Connie shouted over her shoulder to me. "Out of shape, my love."

I growled and sped up, desperate to get my hands on my wife's delicious curves. Her arse wiggled deliciously at me from behind the scrap of red cotton hiding her gorgeous backside from me. "Be careful!" I shouted back. "Don't forget Annie is with Bullet and Panther for the night. You, my love, are all mine when the sun goes down. And unfortunately," I chuckled when I pounced on them both and brought us all tumbling into the softness of the sand, "you're going to be punished for that smart remark."

Annie took off running up the beach as I captured Connie beneath me and pinned her down. "I'll get help!" she shouted before Panther screamed at her and chased her in the opposite direction.

Connie rolled her eyes then winked. "Annie seems to think I need help."

I snorted, burying my face in her neck and tickling her soft skin with my stubble, raking it up and down until she slapped me and squirmed underneath me. "Scream for help, if you dare." I chuckled.

She grabbed my hair and moved my face to hers. "Help me," she whispered. "I'm being devoured by a huge fat guy."

"You cheeky bitch!"

She laughed loudly when I rolled her beneath me, checked up the beach to see if Annie was in sight, then brought my hand down sharply on her arse. She gasped, the dirty little minx. "Again?"

"Oh God, yes please," she panted as she lifted her backside slightly.

"Jesus H Christ!" Bullet huffed as she skipped into the water beside us. "Control yourselves."

"You're only jealous 'cos you don't get any of this," Connie joked, cupping her very nice tits in her hands and wiggling them.

Bullet rolled her eyes. "Only 'cos I can't get fucking near you with this humungous belly."

"Aww," Connie cooed as she managed to pull out of my hold to stroke Bullet's belly as she paddled beside her best friend. Bloody women.

Lying on my back, I looked up at the bright blue sky, marvelling at the calm in my chest as the warm waters rolled over my toes. The last year had been the most challenging of my life, but the very best. I wanted to repeat every single minute of it.

We were happy, and every time I saw the perfect smile on Connie's face, I finally knew I had achieved something good. My life had been far from normal; it still wasn't normal, but now we had the house of our dreams, the things we'd longed for, we even had the puppy that we'd promised to Annie. Yet, looking at my wife as she came to lie beside me, I knew that material things didn't matter; she did. Her and my surrogate daughter. They were my life now. I wasn't ashamed to say I'd killed dozens of people. I had tortured, maimed and slaughtered, however now I had something to kill and punish for; my family. I would protect them with my very last breath. If anyone was to threaten our perfect life, a life Connie had only dreamed for in all her suffering, then I wouldn't take another breath until I had torn out their hearts.

"You okay?" she asked as she nuzzled into me.

Annie came bounding over to us and curled up at the other side of me as I opened my arm and pulled her in. Both Connie and Annie grinned at each other from opposite sides of my chest. "I'm happy," I whispered as I sank a kiss into her soft hair. I grimaced at the tightness in my throat, the restriction making my words sound as choked as I felt.

But Connie didn't look at me as though I was a wuss for showing emotion, she looked at me like I'd given her the stars and the moon. She looked at me with every single bit of love she had for me. She smiled and ran her finger across my gruff chin, her eyes shining with devotion.

Feeling another finger on the other side of my face, I

turned to look at Annie who was grinning mischievously as she mimicked her aunt and dramatically stroked my chin. Then sighing with happiness, she turned her face and looked up to the sky. A huge smile covered her face and she shot up.

"Holly!" She clapped her hands in delight when the most delicate blue butterfly fluttered its wings around my little girl. "You came back!"

Connie gasped and stared open-mouthed at the butterfly. "Oh my God," she breathed when from behind the first butterfly the most vibrant yellow one fluttered its large strong wings. They both danced around Annie's head before they shivered in the breeze and flew away.

"Goodbye," Connie whispered beside me as tears streamed down her face and she blew a kiss to the butterflies.

Annie turned to us and grinned. "I've decided what my Phantom tag will be."

Connie coughed and I spluttered at her sudden statement.

"I'm going to be the Blue Butterfly," she declared as she watched the two pairs of gentle wings dance into the sun.

No way was she ever becoming a Phantom.

Yet, as with the rest of my life, Annie showed me just how strong and remarkable she was. She grew into the most beautiful creature ever to grace the earth. And beside Connie and me, she blossomed from her cocoon and emerged as the most formidable assassin ever in the history of all the Phantoms.

The two butterflies visited Connie and Annie on many occasions throughout their lives, but none were ever as significant as that time because at long last, my wife, my beautiful strong wife finally said goodbye. And that was all she'd ever hoped for.

The End

Keep reading for a sneak peak of

THE TEMPTATION OF ANNIE

Book 4 in the Blue Butterfly Series

D H SIDEBOTTOM

Prologue

AUNTIE CONNIE SMILED softly as she sighed heavily and came to sit beside me on the bed, placing a small box beside her on the light grey duvet. "You okay?"

Was I? Would I ever be?

"Strangely, yes," I answered truthfully as I stared down at my hands, turning them over as if I expected them to still be covered in blood. She gripped hold of them tightly and I looked up to her face. She looked sad, pained even. Her teeth were worrying her bottom lip as her throat dipped with her anguish.

"The first is always the worst, Annie, but I won't lie and say it doesn't get easier."

"How can it ever get easier?" Nothing made sense in my head. But it wasn't the guilt or the disgust eating me up, it was the fact that I didn't feel either of those emotions that made my gut clench with nausea. "How can I even feel like this?"

Connie smiled, her eyes foretelling her love for me. She had watched me grow into a twenty one year old. She had nurtured me like a mother, taught me right from wrong, and last night she had trained me exactly how to gut a man with the minimum outflow of blood.

"You're so very much like your mother, Annie." Her sadness was extreme, the potency of it swallowing my tears and forcing my dry eyes to blink in effort to release the wetness that never came. Since I was four, the day I had cried at the death of my father I had never shed a tear again. It wasn't that I was heartless, or even cold, it was just a case of nothing could ever match the pain from that day. Don't get me wrong, I hadn't suffered as a child, or missed out on anything, Connie and Isaac had loved me enough for what I had lost from the death of my parents, yet a part of me would never be filled with their absence.

I smiled in reply to her words but when she reached out to me with something in her hands, my mouth dried and the heartache tripled with what my eyes witnessed.

"Your father's journal," Connie whispered as we both stared at it. "I wanted to give it to you so many times but it never quite felt right. But now, now you'll understand."

Tentatively I took it from her, the feel of it heavy in my hands, and my soul. "Have you read it?"

She nodded. "Yes. It's not light reading Ann, in fact it's fucking heart wrenching at times, and nauseating at others, but maybe it will help you to accept who you are." As if reluctant, she pulled something else out of the box she had carried in. She stared down at a folded piece of material and my heart twisted when a lone tear rolled down her cheek. Slowly, she raised it to her face and inhaled its scent, then passed it to me. "And this was something very dear to your mother. At first I didn't understand how significant it was to her, until I read Daniel's journal."

The soft pink cotton opened in my hands until a long pink

slip lay across my lap. "This was my mother's?"

Connie nodded, her eyes now flooding with her tears but still she smiled. "Yes." Saying nothing else, she gently kissed the top of my head then left me alone.

Reaching for the journal, I flicked through the pages until it opened at a specific point.

13th January 2009

My heart stilled today for the very first time in the entirety of my life. Mae was wearing the pink slip left out for her, whether it was herself or Pauline that dressed her I am unsure, but my eyes no longer saw the little lamb as a provision for money, but as a stunning creature. Her scar is disregarded by my eyes, and my soul, her exquisite beauty the only thing I saw today.

The Temptation of Annie
The final book in the Blue Butterfly series

Coming early 2016

Coming Soon

Night Fires

An erotic romance novel

D H SIDEBOTTOM

Prologue

The vicar didn't make any sense, his mouth moved but foreign words filled my ears, my brain unable to decode the poetic way he spoke. All I heard was the creak of the wood when my brother's coffin landed on top of my parents with a soft thud.

A faint puff of air left me and I pulled my black wool coat tighter around me as I shivered against the cold wind that blew through the cemetery. Snow covered the grass, disguising the only thing of colour around me, nothing but grey and more grey enveloped me.

Faint sobs from the other mourners filtered in but I couldn't join them, the walls that had built around me refused to allow my own despair to be vocal. Loneliness was all that surrounded me. Loneliness and numbness. And the eternal scent of smoke – and death.

The vicar's eyes were fixed on me as if awaiting for some sort of acknowledgment. Not understanding, or caring, I nodded vaguely to him, hoping that was enough. It seemed to be when he nodded to the men stood beside the six foot square of hollow earth and they slowly started to lower the small coffin. The final coffin. My eyes watched but my heart refused to. All I could think was how all they all managed to fit into such a small hole.

I turned to look to the side when a man came to stand beside me. Mutely, I lifted a questioning brow to him but he shook his head slowly, sadly, and returned his gaze to my family descending below the ground. Taking my hand, he leaned towards me. "I promise, Alice. Before I go I will give you a smile once again."

I didn't answer him. For one, I couldn't take my eyes away from my dead family, and for two, I didn't hold the same confidence.

Without waiting for the service to finish, I dropped Brandon's hand and walked towards the final resting place of the only people I loved and blew them a final kiss.

"Look after them Billy. I love you all. Forever."

Dove

An erotic thriller by D H Sidebottom

After her mother abandoned her when she was just fourteen, Dove fled the only life she'd known with her younger sister, Serenity, frightened that the authorities would tear them both apart.

Leaving behind a life of poverty and constant hardship with the group of traveller's she had grown up with, Dove has no choice but to turn to a life of debauchery and prostitution to feed their bellies and provide them with shelter and security.

Span forwards ten years and life is so very different. Dove, now a world famous, high class escort receives a job that will change her life forever.

Her once best friend and fellow traveller, Flick O'Kane, now a billionaire Hollywood star, hires Dove to accompany him to a charity ball, unaware just who exactly this premium whore really is.

Both their lives come together in an explosion of sex, drugs and secrets. The friendship they once held close is about to be tested when their past threatens to rip them both apart and endangers not just their own lives but the very life Dove has broken her own soul for – Serenity's.

WARNING
This story is not for the fainthearted. It includes scenes of non-consensual sex, forced prostitution, drug abuse and violence.

COMING WINTER 2015

Coming October 2015

My Diary By Mason Fox

A Heart of Stone Novel
By D H Sidebottom

21st august 1993

Aged 14

They were at it again today. Arguing. His voice grates on my nerves, hers makes my ear drums squeal. What the hell is it with my mother? Why does she put up with his sick and twisted demands just in the name of marriage?

Marriage – what a fucking farce. Why the hell would you want to spend the rest of your life with one person? Christ, that's a scary thought.

Saying that, my father doesn't stick to one woman, never has. Although his latest freaky demand still makes my skin crawl. I know most of my mates think he's cool, and are jealous that my dad is who he is, but fuck, why I'd wanna watch his dick slip into a whore is beyond me.

I just stared at him yesterday when he'd told me to follow him into his 'office'. 'Office' – it's a fucking building down the garden where he deals with 'business'. A square concrete structure that contains washable floors that are easily bleached to remove 'evidence' and a wrought iron bed placed to one side of the room. Chains and ropes dangle from the ceiling above it. But it's an upgrade from the wooden shed he used to have.

He said I was old enough now I am 14 and 'man' enough to see what men should be about. 'Men' – that's a fucking laugh. He's not a man, he's a fucking sick bastard.

What 'normal' 14 year old is made to stand and watch his father tie up a young girl? Strip her naked, spit on her, degrade her? My sick eyes had dropped to watch his cock slide into the ass of a woman who obviously enjoyed being degraded and fucked by someone who doesn't give a fucking damn whether she's enjoying it or not?

My treacherous cock had enjoyed it though, but my stomach had twisted at the thought that watching my dad fuck had turned me on. Shit, did that make me a perv?

Shit! I'm fucking gagging again now.

I'm off for a shower, see if I can scrub the whore's scent off me. What the fuck had I been thinking? But I'd been too fucking horny that I couldn't resist when my father had pulled out of her, passed me a condom, said 'Happy birthday' and told me it was time I lost my virginity.

I'm as repulsive as he is!

Fuck! FUCK!

TEN

By Ker Dukey

Ten years old I fell in love
Ten years was the price of that love
Ten years later our world's re-collide

Alexandria (Alex)

My brother Jonah was possessive when it came to the things he owned; this unfortunately included the people in his life. The forbidden love between his best friend and me was just that... forbidden.

Our families were from different walks of life and as a sheriff's daughter being with a Moore's kid would never be tolerated. To my parents their son and Dalton Moore were on different paths and their friendship would end as soon as college began but it was my brother who had a craving for trouble. He was always looking for danger, committing petty crimes and getting away with it because Dalton would take the fall, blackening his already stained name. When Jonah found out we broke the rules by loving each other, his consequences impacted us all with immeasurable suffering.

> Betrayal comes with a debt and it would be
> paid by all of us.
> One with their heart,
> one with their mind
> and one would pay in blood.

Acknowledgements

As usual, a huge thank you to my family, Vic and Nikki Nut; your love and loyalty keep me going in the long lonely nights, and none of this would as much fun without you.

My beautiful betas; you make Connie and Isaac who they are, and your support is never taken for granted. Thank you ladies!!

To Kyra, my editor; thank you so much for making my shit readable… and for all your comments that make me smile and chuckle.

Stacey, Champagne Formats; My words make the story but your skill makes them beautiful… Thank you!!

To Ker Dukey, my mind's soulmate; Thank you for pushing me to be my best, without you this crazy world wouldn't quite be as crazy, and that is utterly unthinkable!! ;)

And to you, the reader; there's only one thing to say really… "Without you, I wouldn't be here, doing what I love. So my heart and soul are yours!!

Printed in Great Britain
by Amazon.co.uk, Ltd.,
Marston Gate.